FREEFALL TO DESIRE

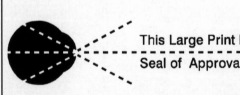

This Large Print Book carries the
Seal of Approval of N.A.V.H.

FREEFALL TO DESIRE

KAYLA PERRIN

THORNDIKE PRESS
A part of Gale, Cengage Learning

Detroit • New York • San Francisco • New Haven, Conn • Waterville, Maine • London

Copyright © 2011 by Kayla Perrin.
Thorndike Press, a part of Gale, Cengage Learning.

Thorndike Press® Large Print African-American.
The text of this Large Print edition is unabridged.
Other aspects of the book may vary from the original edition.
Set in 16 pt. Plantin.

LIBRARY OF CONGRESS CATALOGING-IN-PUBLICATION DATA

Perrin, Kayla.
 Freefall to desire / by Kayla Perrin. — Large print ed.
  p. cm. — (Thorndike Press large print African-American)
 ISBN-13: 978-1-4104-3587-3 (hardcover)
 ISBN-10: 1-4104-3587-3 (hardcover)
 1. African Americans—Fiction. 2. Large type books. I. Title.
PR9199.3.P434F74 2011
8137'.54—dc22   2010051970

Published in 2011 by arrangement with Harlequin Books S.A.

Printed in Mexico
1 2 3 4 5 6 7 15 14 13 12 11

This book is dedicated to Lady Sharon.
Talented fashion designer.
Dedicated mother.
Great friend. I admire how
you're going after your
dreams, making them a reality.
And proving that it's
never too late. God bless you,
my friend!

DEAR READER

After *Island Fantasy,* many of you asked me to write a story for Shayna's sister, Brianne. I'm pleased to tell you that I have, and *Free-fall to Desire* is the result.

If you've enjoyed reading my stories over the years, you'll know that I often infuse elements of intrigue into my books. I love the heightened emotions of a romance combined with intrigue. Because when the world around the characters is falling apart and they're most vulnerable, they're often more likely to let go and seize love in an unguarded way. It's spontaneous and raw and thrilling!

I knew before I set out to write Brianne's story that I wanted there to be an unsolved mystery in the book. One that would force her to work closely with someone from her past and one that would give her a second chance at love. So when Brianne, who has guarded her heart since losing her fiancé, suddenly finds herself in love's grip — especially when she least expects it — it is sweeter and more intense than anything she has ever experienced. Because this time, it's real.

Please let me know how you enjoyed Brianne and Alex's story by emailing me at kayla@kaylaperrin.com or by contacting me on Facebook or Twitter. Up next will be Selena's story, a friend of Brianne's you'll meet briefly in this book. I plan to continue writing stories that feature friends and family of my characters, because I know how much you love them.

Until next time,
Kayla

PROLOGUE

Brianne Kenyon held her breath, her eyes locking with Alex Thorpe's the moment he stepped into the lobby. For two long hours she had been waiting for his return, praying every second of that time for the best possible outcome. But one look at the defeated expression on his face and she knew that the news was not good.

She rose from the sofa where she and her sister, Shayna, had been sitting and waiting by the cozy fireplace — but nothing about their visit to British Columbia was cozy.

"Nothing?" she asked Alex as he reached her. "No sign of him?"

He ran a hand over his head, emitting a groan of frustration. "Brianne, I'm sorry."

"But how can that be possible?" she asked. "There has to be *something. Some* sign of him on the mountain."

"The Rockies are vast, Brianne," Alex explained. "He could be anywhere."

Brianne stared at Alex, willing him to say something that would give her hope. Not the spiel she'd heard from the Canadian authorities over the last five days.

"But," he continued, then stopped.

"But what?" Brianne asked quickly. She felt her sister slip her arm around her waist, offering support. "There is something. What is it?"

"It . . . it's not good."

Brianne's stomach sank. She felt nauseous. But she had to know. Good or bad. "Tell me."

"The search team . . . they found something," Alex explained slowly. "Carter's jacket. It was torn . . . and . . . bloody."

"It might not be Carter's," Brianne said without hesitation.

"It was. After I described to them what Carter was wearing that day, they were able to identify the jacket as his. And the moment they showed it to me, I confirmed it." Alex paused. "It's bad enough to be out there in this weather, but without a jacket?" His statement hung in the air, heavy and ominous.

Brianne's brain tried to process the news. She couldn't speak.

"What are you saying?" Shayna asked. "Do the authorities think that Carter —"

10

"They don't want to jump to conclusions," Alex interjected. "But at the very least, they figure Carter's hurt. The blood could mean that he fell . . . or that he was attacked by an animal."

"What kind of animal?" Shayna asked.

Brianne moved away from her sister then, stepping in the direction of the fire. But it did nothing to warm her. She felt cold from the inside out.

"A wolf," Alex said. "Maybe a cougar."

A cougar? God help her. Brianne's knees buckled then, and she faltered. But strong arms wrapped around her waist before she could collapse onto the floor.

Alex held her up. "Brianne, are you okay?"

A wolf. Maybe a cougar . . . No, she wasn't okay.

"Brianne?"

Brianne broke down and cried. Cried at the reality that her fiancé was lost in the middle of the Rockies, left to fend for himself in horrendous conditions.

In six days he hadn't turned up. Five days of searching had produced no sign of him — until now.

A wolf. Maybe a cougar . . .

"Damn, Brianne. I hate this." Alex cradled her head against his chest. She gripped his arms, holding on to him as she rode through

11

the turbulent emotional wave.

After about two minutes, she shook her head and eased backward. "No. I won't believe that he's anything other than okay. Carter is strong. You know how strong he is. He's got to be fine."

"Brianne —"

"Don't tell me I'm wrong," she snapped. One minute she'd been bawling, the next biting Alex's head off. She wanted this all to end.

"Brianne, listen to me," Alex said. "I know exactly how you're feeling. But it's worse than we want to think."

"Everything will be fine when they find Carter," Brianne said, refusing to give in to despair.

"They're not going to find him," Alex said.

"How can you say that?" She felt a spurt of anger. "Why are you giving up already?"

"Because they're calling off the search," Alex answered matter-of-factly.

Brianne's body went rigid. She looked up at Alex in confusion. "How can they call off the search? Carter's still lost!"

"I wish it wasn't the case, Brianne. God knows I do. But they've searched for five full days, and the snow has continued to fall, covering any possible tracks. It was a fluke they found his jacket. After all this time out there, they think it's really unlikely —"

"I don't care what they think," Brianne interrupted before Alex could say the words she didn't want to hear. "They found his jacket, so they know he's hurt. He's got to be close by. It's critical that they keep searching so they can find him now!"

"I agree with you," Alex said.

"Then do something!" Brianne yelled, not meaning to, but unable to stop herself. People in the hotel lobby looked in her direction. She knew they were wondering what was going on, but she didn't care. She would make as big a scene as necessary if it got her the results she wanted.

Alex raised his hands in a helpless gesture and then let them fall against his thighs. "What can I do?"

Brianne shook her head in disbelief. "He's your best friend and you're giving up on him." She turned around and marched back to the sofa where she'd left her coat. "Fine. If the authorities are giving up the search, then I have to find Carter."

"Brianne, you can't go out there."

Ignoring Alex, she shoved her arms into the ultrawarm parka she'd bought. "Someone has to!"

"Brianne," Shayna said gently. "If the

authorities can't find Carter . . ."

"No, don't say it. Please, Shayna. *Don't say it.*"

And then she started for the door.

Alex reached her before she could step outside. "Don't be foolish, Brianne. Carter wouldn't want you to get lost, too."

And as she met Alex's gaze, saw the pain she was feeling shimmering in his eyes, she knew he was right.

There was nothing she could do.

Her knees giving way again, she reached out and gripped Alex's forearms. Gripped them for dear life as emotion overwhelmed her.

This time when she cried, she couldn't stop the tears. Because she had most likely lost the love of her life. The man she was supposed to marry next year.

And her life would never be the same.

CHAPTER 1

Three years later . . .

Brianne held the heavy silver picture frame with both hands, staring fondly at the photo of the smiling couple behind the glass.

Three years, she thought. *Three years since you've been gone.*

Brianne wore an ear-to-ear grin in the picture, more giggle than smile. She'd been giddy with happiness as she'd posed with Carter Smith, the man who'd stolen her heart at a point when she hadn't expected to fall in love. She and Carter were standing against a palm tree, the picturesque stretch of sand and blue water in Hawaii behind them. Even if Brianne and Carter hadn't been in Maui for a romantic vacation, she would have remembered exactly when the photo had been taken.

It had been taken the day Carter had proposed to her.

The helicopter ride Carter had booked for

them turned into the most memorable moment of all when he'd surprised Brianne with an exquisite cushion-cut diamond engagement ring. Soaring over a volcano, Carter had asked Brianne to marry him, and she had enthusiastically said yes. Emotionally, she'd been higher than any cloud, expecting that nothing would happen to destroy the happiness she'd been feeling at the time. Brianne had been in love and looking forward to a wonderful life with the man of her dreams. At the time, she couldn't imagine anything ever going wrong.

But things had gone wrong. Barely two months after they'd gotten engaged. All at once, everything had changed.

Brianne's eyes misted as she regarded the photo of her and Carter in happier times. It was still hard to believe what had happened, much less accept it.

And yet, here she was, without Carter. Today was the three-year anniversary since that tragic, cold day in the Rocky Mountains.

Gone. In an instant. Carter Smith had simply vanished.

That was the hardest part to bear, the not knowing if he was alive or dead.

The authorities had been of a different opinion than Brianne. No, they hadn't found Carter's body, but they had found remnants of the torn and bloodied jacket he'd been wearing. Given that finding, coupled with the unexpected snowstorm, they'd surmised that Carter had lost his way on the mountain and that the unthinkable had happened. Months later, hikers had stumbled upon Carter's backpack — which included his passport — approximately ten miles from the spot where they'd found his jacket. That had solidified the opinion that he had died.

Brianne could not deny that the snowstorm had likely led to Carter getting lost. But what she did not accept — could not accept — was that the man who had so enthusiastically loved the outdoors and could cope in almost any circumstance could have become a victim of nature. The authorities believed one of two possibilities: the first was that Carter had died during the snowstorm and his remains had been eaten by animals. The second possibility was even worse to imagine — that Carter had been attacked and killed by hungry wildlife while alive.

Brianne shuddered. She didn't want to let her mind go there. Thinking that Carter had died was bad enough, but imagining that his body had been eaten . . . That part was too much to contemplate. And yet, she had nightmares about exactly that.

But despite the nightmares, Brianne had been able to cling to some hope. The hope that since there had been no body, maybe Carter was still alive.

Before Carter's disappearance, Brianne had seen stories on the news about people who had been missing for years, only to turn up unexpectedly one day suffering from amnesia. After Carter's disappearance, she had become addicted to such stories. Four months after Carter was gone, she broke down and bawled when she saw a story on the news about a man in Oregon who had survived some mishap in the wilderness and had resurfaced across the country a year later. Brianne believed fervently that this would be the news she would one day get regarding Carter.

Shayna didn't believe Carter was alive. Nor did anyone else in her family. But how could Brianne allow herself to think that Carter was dead when it was just as possible that he was alive somewhere, not knowing who he was and therefore unable to get back to her?

Perhaps she was naive to hope. But she hadn't wanted to give up. Now, however, on the three-year anniversary of Carter's disappearance, she was wondering if she had simply been lying to herself the entire time.

Just because you wished something was true didn't make it so.

After three years, Brianne needed some sort of closure, and that closure would not come by hanging on to the hope that Carter might return. As hard as it was going to be, she had to say a final goodbye to him.

If Carter had not returned yet, it was likely that he never would. Her sister, Shayna, had tried to encourage her to move on for her own sanity.

Brianne knew that Shayna was right. Moving on was truly the only way she would ever heal. Sometimes in life bad things happened. This was one of those times.

Brianne replaced the framed photo on her dresser and drew in a deep breath in an attempt to calm her frayed nerves. Perhaps a trip to the Rockies would help her get closure. She had felt helpless at the time when Carter was lost. The authorities had searched the mountains, as had Alex Thorpe — Carter's best friend, who had accompanied him on the ill-fated hiking trip. Brianne had gone crazy with worry at a nearby hotel, waiting for word, unable to do anything to aid in the search. All she could do was pray.

There had been a memorial service organized by Carter's family, held at the Rockies. But Brianne had stubbornly refused to attend and had instead returned home. One year later, in Buffalo, she had attended the memorial service marking the one-year anniversary of Carter's disappearance. She had done so out of respect for Carter's family rather than a desire to move on, but she had been angry at almost everyone in attendance — at all the people who had so quickly chosen to believe that their friend and family member was not coming back.

Before, Brianne had doggedly not wanted to give in to the belief that Carter was dead, as if just wishing him alive would influence reality.

Now she had to move on. And maybe the only way to do that was to go to the last place Carter had been seen alive. Have her own private memorial for Carter at the Rockies and bid him a final goodbye.

As she made her way downstairs to the kitchen, the idea felt right. Yes, she would plan a trip to British Columbia. It would be nice to go with Shayna, but her sister had just gotten married, and she and her new husband, Donovan, were still honeymooning in Jamaica. Brianne's parents were also out of town, having decided to spend an extra week in Jamaica as well.

There was no reason Brianne couldn't go to British Columbia alone. In fact, maybe that was best. A quiet time for reflection, to make peace with what had happened.

Brianne was a manager at Scented Suds, a store that sold a variety of luxury body soaps and lotions. As a manager, she was entitled to several weeks of vacation per year. But she had just returned from Jamaica two days ago and didn't like the idea of requesting more time off without much notice. However, it was necessary. Alexis, the store's assistant manager, would certainly be able to manage the store in her absence. Brianne would have to run the request by Marlene, the district manager. She didn't doubt that Marlene — who knew firsthand the stress Brianne had gone through when Carter had disappeared — would allow her this additional time off.

Brianne got herself a low-fat granola bar and a bottle of water from the kitchen and then went back up to her room, where she booted up her laptop. The smart thing would be to check for flights and find out when it was most economically feasible to head to Canada. Then she could call Marlene with a definite time frame.

It would have been nice to be there today, the official anniversary. But the thought had come to Brianne too late. The truth was, it was a thought she hadn't even considered. Perhaps it was seeing her sister and Donovan, so much in love on their wedding day, that was leading her to take that final step toward closure.

Three years had passed. It was time she made peace with the fact that Carter wasn't coming back.

She was only twenty-seven. Far too young to accept that she would never get married. She couldn't even imagine falling in love with someone else, but Brianne knew that time healed all wounds. One day, she would fall in love again.

While she couldn't be at the Rockies today, Brianne had waited three years to get to the point where she finally felt like she could move on. She could wait a week or so more.

And for her, moving on meant more than accepting that Carter wasn't coming back. It was letting go of the anger she felt toward Carter's best friend, Alex. Alex had been with Carter that fateful day, and *he* had come out of the mountain alive. Her rational brain knew that Alex wasn't responsible for what had happened to Carter, but he had never satisfactorily explained *why* he had gotten off the mountain and Carter had not.

Brianne had been looking for answers — something she'd made very clear to Alex on the few occasions that they'd spoken. Now, she was beginning to consider just how hard the whole ordeal must have been for Alex. To be the one who survived, while his friend had not. He had probably replayed the day's events over and over in his head, wondering if there was one thing he could have done differently that would have changed the outcome. Brianne certainly had — and she hadn't even been on the trip.

She wasn't the only one who'd lost someone that cold November day. Alex Thorpe had lost a friend and business partner, and the guilt he felt because he hadn't been able to save Carter had likely eaten at him over the years.

Brianne poised her fingers over the keyboard, ready to type. But then she thought she heard the doorbell.

Had she?

She paused, straining to listen. A few seconds later, she knew she had heard correctly when the doorbell sounded again.

She got up from the small desk in the corner of her room, wondering who might be here. It was early evening, just after six, but dark outside. She didn't expect solicitors, nor a delivery person. Maybe it was her best friend, Kim, whom she'd spoken to earlier, coming to help get her mind off of the past.

Brianne hurried downstairs and then looked through the peephole as she always did before swinging the door open. But what she saw there made her reel backward.

Rather, *who* she saw there.

She was flabbergasted.

It may have been dark, but she knew her eyes were not deceiving her. Even if never in a million years did she expect to see *him.*

Indeed, two full years had passed since she'd laid eyes on him.

And yet, it made perfect sense that he was here. He, like she, had been forever affected by what had happened on this day three years ago.

The doorbell sounded again. Slowly, Brianne unlocked and opened the door. And there stood Alex Thorpe, on her small front porch, with a serious expression on his face.

And though Brianne had told herself only moments ago that she should hold no anger toward him, it flared again. As irrational as it was, Alex was a physical outlet for her pain and frustration. A person she could blame for something that had been out of everyone's control.

"Brianne." Alex spoke her name, as serious as the expression on his face.

Brianne said nothing. She didn't know what to say. The last time she and Alex had spoken, two years ago exactly, he'd gotten her so angry she'd stormed off.

"It's been a year, Brianne. There's been no sign of him. No action in any of his bank accounts. And he was never documented crossing the border back into the States. Do you really expect Carter to walk back into your life? What are you hanging on to?"

And Brianne realized, in that instant, why she'd been so angry with Alex over the past couple of years. At first, she had thought it was because Alex had been Carter's partner in crime — the guy Carter always went off with on his thrill-seeking adventures. From sky-diving to extreme skiing to base jumping off of buildings . . . to hiking mountains in bad weather. It had been easy to think that if Alex had refused to go with Carter, Carter might not have gotten lost on that mountain.

But it was more than that, and Brianne now knew why. Alex had been Carter's best friend, and yet he had so easily given up on him. Like the others who wanted to declare him dead and move on, Alex had done the very same thing.

But as a best friend, she had expected him to want to do all in his power to find Carter. To travel to the ends of the earth, if that was necessary. To leave no stone unturned, as the saying went. Instead, on the one-year anniversary of Carter's disappearance, Alex had told her that she was foolishly hanging on to hope.

"I'm holding on to our love!" Brianne had shouted at him outside the church, not meaning to yell. "And what exactly happened on the mountain? How did you and Carter get separated? How is it that you came off of the mountain alive, but he didn't?"

Alex hadn't answered the question, just advised her that it was time for her to accept reality. That was when Brianne had stormed off, away from Alex Thorpe, not caring if she never saw him again.

And yet here he was, on her doorstep two years later.

"You shouldn't be here," she said to him now. She might have resolved to let go of her anger toward him, but him being here was stirring up the uncertainty and helplessness she'd felt surrounding Carter's disappearance. If they spoke again, it had to be when she was ready. When she could talk to him without the weight of Carter's disappearance between them.

"I know you don't want to see me," Alex said, his voice low. "And trust me, I wouldn't be here if this wasn't important. But what I have to say . . . it needed to be in person." He paused for a moment, huddling into his leather jacket as a cold breeze swirled. "Can we talk inside?"

Brianne looked beyond him to the late-model, high-end Mercedes parked at her sidewalk. It was black and sparkled beneath the streetlights. She knew it was his — which meant he'd driven here.

"I thought you were in Phoenix," Brianne said. Word was, Alex had moved there to open up another store in the sporting goods chain he and Carter had started. Life and business had gone on for him — something else that irked Brianne, even if it was irrational to expect anything else.

"I was, but I'm back. Look, it's pretty cold outside. Can I come in?"

Brianne wanted to say no. She wanted to tell him that it hurt too much to see him, especially today. That he should leave and come back later — or better yet, not at all.

But the fact that he was here spoke volumes. And even though his presence reminded her of what had happened three years ago, it also reminded her of something else. That they'd once been friends.

Maybe Alex was here to make amends with another person who had loved Carter dearly. Wasn't it time they started talking again? Rationally, she knew that Carter wouldn't have wanted them upset with each other, as they were that day two years ago.

That thought filling her mind, Brianne stepped backward and held the door open. "All right," she said softly, her tone guarded. "You can come in."

Alex bent his head slightly as he entered the house. He was tall — six foot four, a little taller than the height of the doorframe of the prewar house. His body was in the same muscular form Brianne remembered from the past. No surprise there. In addition to their thrill-seeking, both Alex and Carter had been active in a variety of sports — cycling, kickboxing, basketball. They'd liked to spend hours on the weekends playing a variety of sports, keeping their bodies perfectly toned. Their love of sport had led them to open their first sporting goods store in downtown Buffalo, and then a second in Amherst and a third in Niagara Falls. Two men, best friends since childhood, had worked hard to achieve the American dream and had succeeded.

But that dream had been marred with the

death of one half of the business.

Brianne looked at Alex then — really stared at him. And noted that his attractive face was marred with a scowl. Again, it struck her that he had probably been carrying around an enormous amount of guilt. She wondered if he had smiled in the last three years.

"We can chat in here," Brianne said, gesturing to the sitting room near the front door. She led the way into the room, turning on the lights as she did, then took a seat on one of the sofas. Alex folded his tall frame into the lounge chair opposite her.

Just looking at him, Brianne felt regret. How had they lost not only Carter but their friendship? In fact, when Brianne had walked into their sporting goods store, she had noticed Alex first. Noticed his extreme good looks and warm smile. Then out of nowhere, Carter had appeared and offered to help her. She'd been shopping for a bike, and Carter had helped her try a number of them in order to find the one best suited to her. It had been clear to her that Carter was spending more time with her than necessary. He had been flirting, and Brianne — unused to that kind of attention — had been flattered. The rest, as they say, was history. She'd fallen for Carter, but she'd also become friends with Alex. Now she regretted that the death of Carter had also led to the death of their bond.

"I'm glad you came to see me," she said before he could speak. "I guess it's about time we . . . talk again." Her emotions were all over the place — from anger to regret and now to empathy — but she supposed that was to be expected. Empathy was now morphing into a dull ache of pain. Pain over Carter's loss, but also pain over the fact that she'd lost Alex's friendship.

Alex nodded. His expression was still grim, making Brianne wonder if the pain for him was as intense as when Carter had disappeared into that storm.

"I never should have said those things I said to you," she continued. "I know it wasn't your fault. It was the grief talking."

"We both lost someone we cared about, but we shouldn't have lost our friendship," Brianne went on when Alex said nothing. "Thank you for being the one with the courage to make the first move."

When Alex still didn't speak, it struck Brianne that for a man who'd shown up on her door claiming that they needed to talk, he was being strangely silent.

Instead he sighed, the heavy sound filling the quiet room.

And that's when she understood that something was seriously wrong. That Alex hadn't shown up to talk about mending their friendship.

"Oh, dear God in heaven." Brianne leaned forward, clutching her stomach as it roiled. Though she'd known the news would come one day, she suddenly wasn't prepared for it. Carter's remains must have been found. After all this time, his bones had been discovered and tested for DNA and —

"Brianne." Alex paused. Sighed. Then he forged ahead. "There's no real way to say this —"

"They found him," she said, the finality of the words too hard to wrap her mind around. Three years of not knowing, and now —

"He's not dead."

Brianne looked up at Alex, the tears that had formed in her eyes blurring his image. Certainly she hadn't heard him correctly. "Wh— what did you say?"

"All this time, you didn't believe it. You didn't believe he was dead."

Another pause. Brianne continued to stare at Alex, not understanding.

And then he said the words she never thought he would ever utter. "Brianne, I

think you were right all along. I think Carter's alive."

CHAPTER 2

If Alex had just up and slapped her, Brianne would have been less surprised.

She gaped at Alex, certain she had not heard him correctly. "What did you say?"

"Unbelievable, right? But I think it's possible Carter didn't die three years ago."

"You think . . . you think Carter is . . ." Brianne couldn't even say it. So long she had wanted to believe it. But she didn't want to get her hopes up, only to be wrong.

"I know," Alex said. "After all this time, it sounds crazy. Impossible. But I think . . . I really think Carter's alive."

Seconds of silence passed. Alex stared at her, and she stared back at him in utter bewilderment. "But . . . but why have you changed your mind?" she finally asked. "I don't understand. You were certain he was dead. That's what you told me two years ago." Brianne was confused and felt like she was in a turbulent sea, being rocked around

33

by waves with nothing to cling to for support.

Alex didn't speak, and Brianne got the sense that even he wasn't sure of the answer. But there had to be a reason for the about-face.

"You can't just come here and tell me that you think Carter is alive." *Only for this to be some misplaced speculation.* "Not after three years."

"I saw something on television," Alex began slowly.

"Something on television?" Brianne repeated, already doubting that what he was about to say could change her mind about what she had come to accept. "What, a documentary about people going missing the way Carter did? I saw those, too, and at the end of the day —"

"Hear me out," Alex said. "You'll understand."

"Okay." Obviously the fact that Alex was here meant he thought he had good reason to believe Carter was alive.

"You know Carter and I were into extreme sports."

Did she ever. It was one of the reasons she hadn't been able to forgive Alex, figuring that had he not been Carter's partner in crime, her fiancé might still be alive. "What

34

did you see?"

"A few weeks ago, there was an event called the Fall Cycle Scene — four days of intense motorcycle racing at the Daytona Speedway. It's exactly the kind of thing Carter would have enjoyed. I was watching on a Sunday afternoon, and I thought . . ." He glanced away momentarily before meeting her gaze once more. "I'm pretty sure I saw Carter in the crowd."

Even though she hadn't wanted to, Brianne had begun to hope. But Alex's explanation deflated that hope. "A face in the crowd?"

"Not just in the crowd. It was more than a quick clip of some face in the distance. The guy I'm sure was Carter was with one of the racers, a guy named Dean Knight, who is based out of Daytona. When Dean won his race, the cameras were all over him. And that's when I saw Carter, congratulating Dean on the track. High-fiving him, patting him on the back. The whole nine yards. In fact, it looked to me like Carter was a part of Dean's team."

"Which would be easy enough to check out," Brianne said. "A call to this Dean Knight —"

"That's the problem. I got in touch with Dean's people, left a message for him and he called me back. He said he doesn't know a Carter Smith."

Brianne frowned. "So you're wrong." Why had he bothered to get her hopes up?

"Yeah, I accepted that. For about a week. But I kept thinking about the image I saw. The smile on the guy's face, the way he moved. Carter and I were best friends for fifteen years. I'd know him *anywhere.* His hair was different, but I'm ninety percent positive that that was him."

Carter. Alive. The words Brianne had wanted to hear for so long. But this wasn't proof. This was . . . it was hope on Alex's part. A best friend trying — as she had — to cling to a thread of possibility.

"Alex, this all sounds crazy. It — it can't be true. A face in the crowd, someone who looked liked Carter . . ." She shrugged help-lessly.

"It's more than that," Alex said. "Yes, it sounds crazy, but my gut says it was him." He paused, stared at Brianne for a long mo-ment. "And I was thinking — hoping — that maybe we can work together to find him."

Alex saw the way the expression on Bri-anne's face changed from stunned to hope-ful. It was subtle. She was still confused and overwhelmed — that was also evident in her expression — but there was definitely a glint of hope in her eyes.

And for that he felt a little bad.

Make that a whole lot of bad.

He didn't want to get her hopes up only to shatter them, but he knew no other way to handle this delicate situation. He had contemplated coming here and telling her everything he suspected, but each time he considered it, he knew he couldn't. Brianne would probably come to the same conclusion he had and react angrily — which would be understandable — but then she would have wanted nothing more to do with Carter. Having lived without him for three years, she would no doubt close the book on him and move on.

She certainly wouldn't want to help look for him.

No, Alex certainly couldn't tell her the truth — at least not the whole truth — and expect her cooperation.

And right now, to get the answers he needed — no, the answers he *deserved* — he needed her cooperation.

There were times when the ends justified the means, especially when the ends were noble. This was one of those times. Because Carter Smith had stolen something from Alex, something that meant the world to him. Plain and simple, he needed it back.

Alex would be there for Brianne in the aftermath of what would undoubtedly happen, would deal with her wrath and help her through the resulting pain. Because there was no other way to handle this. And it was imperative that Alex keep his eye on the end goal.

If there were another way to do this, he would.

Once Alex had spotted Carter on television, he figured tracking him down would be easy. He had contacted Dean Knight and expected that it would be as simple as that — that Dean would say, yeah, he knew Carter Smith, and then Alex would head to Florida to confront his former friend. Instead, Dean had claimed not to know Carter, leaving Alex at square one.

There were two explanations for that. Either Dean was lying, or Carter had lied to Dean about his identity.

Alex figured it was the latter. Because if Carter was alive, then it meant he had faked his death to begin with. Alex would bet his life on that.

"How, exactly, do you think we can find him?" Brianne asked, pulling him from his thoughts.

"By going to Daytona, for one thing.

That's where Dean Knight lives. It's where I saw Carter on television. It could be where he's living right now."

"Maybe. Or maybe not."

"It's the only place I can think of to start the search," Alex said. "We can show Dean his picture, see if he remembers him. Then go from there."

"And you want me along for this?" Brianne asked.

"I figured . . . I figured you'd want to be there."

Brianne nodded. Of course he would expect that. She had hoped for nothing but a reunion with Carter for the past three years. And yet . . .

The idea that Carter was alive was oddly scary. What kind of state was he in mentally? And how would he and Brianne pick up where they'd left off?

"Are you sure, Alex?"

"That I want you to come with me? Yeah."

"No. Are you sure that Carter is alive?"

"One hundred per cent?" Alex shrugged. "I can't say I'm totally certain. All I know is that the guy looked a heck of a lot like Carter. If we all knew Carter to be alive and well, I wouldn't doubt it was him on TV. Absolutely not. But because he's been gone for three years, I can't be totally sure. But my gut . . . I've got to go with it."

"So what I thought all along is possibly true," Brianne said, her voice filling with hope. "He got lost on that mountain. Disoriented. Maybe he fell and hit his head and that caused him to lose his memory. Or he experienced some other trauma."

Brianne slowly rose as she spoke, and the look on her face . . . it was like a stab in Alex's heart. Because he knew that what she was imagining — a happy reunion, the continuation of the future she thought had come to an end — wasn't going to happen.

But until he found Carter, Brianne would have to be in the dark. It was the only way.

"That's a possibility," Carter said, noncommittally. Truthfully, he couldn't rule it out. But in his heart, he didn't believe it. Seeing Carter's face that day, that happy, carefree smile — and seeing him at an event both he and Carter had always enjoyed — well, Alex didn't believe for a second that Carter didn't know who he was. And if he hadn't at first but now did, why not return home? But that was not something he was going to share with Brianne. At least not yet.

"It wouldn't explain how he got across the Canadian border," Brianne said, talking to herself mostly, "but maybe he hiked the

40

Rockies back into America. Anything's possible."

"You've got that right," Alex agreed, a tinge of bitterness in his voice.

But Brianne missed the tone. Facing him, she clasped her hands tightly together. "Alex, I'm shaking."

Alex swallowed, trying not to show any particular emotion. He wanted nothing more than to get up, pull Brianne into his arms and hold her tight.

His eyes roamed over her, from her trembling hands to her trim physique to her widened eyes. Lord, she was a vision. She was thinner. That had changed. She'd obviously spent a good amount of time working out since he'd last seen her. What hadn't changed was that she was still as cute as a button.

It was what he'd thought the first moment he'd seen her. She had walked into the store wearing black pants and a tank top that hugged her beautiful curves. Alex had stepped in her direction, instantly intrigued. But then Carter had made a beeline for her, and that had been that. Alex had lost his chance to pursue anything with Brianne.

"Alex?"

"Hmm?" He looked up at her. He hadn't heard a word she'd said.

"I asked if you really want to do this. Head to Florida?"

He cleared his throat before speaking. "I think it warrants investigation, yes."

Brianne nodded, then bit down on her bottom lip. She looked vulnerable as she stared at some point ahead of her, probably not really seeing anything, just lost in her thoughts.

She suddenly shifted her gaze to his, as though she had caught him staring. Alex moved his eyes.

"What if you're wrong?" she asked softly.

Alex looked at her and shrugged. "Don't you want to know? One way or another?"

"To tell the truth . . . I'm not sure. I . . . I don't know if I could handle getting my hopes up, only to learn that you saw someone who looked like him."

"I know what you mean," Alex said. "But the way things are now, we don't know —"

"And what if he's got this whole other life — which he'd have to, right? A life that doesn't include me?"

"You mean assuming he has amnesia?"

"Yes." She looked scared suddenly, and something inside Alex's gut stirred. "If he's been missing all this time, he must have suffered some type of memory loss. What if he's got a family?" She swallowed. "I don't want . . . I'm not sure I could handle that."

"Even if he's got a new family, he's still got his family back here. Parents who grieved for his loss. Friends. You." He paused, looked at her pointedly. "He deserves to know about the people he's left behind."

Brianne began to pace. "Maybe you're right. But if it does turn out to be Carter, his parents will always be his parents. I'm just a woman he used to love. He's probably forgotten all about me."

Alex stood and walked toward Brianne, stopping only when he was directly in front of her. He placed his hands on her shoulders. "You're more that that," he said, then took a breath, hoping she didn't pick up on the double meaning behind his words. All this time he hadn't seen her, and yet he was still attracted to her.

His best friend's girl.

Former best friend's girl.

"Weren't you the one who didn't want to give up hope?" he asked. "The one who thought for sure that I was wrong, that Carter was out there alive somewhere?" She nodded, but Alex saw pain in her eyes. "Wouldn't you feel better knowing he was alive, even if he's got a new life?"

"I don't know," Brianne said softly.

"Maybe."

"Then we work together. We hit the streets in Florida. We find out if Carter is still alive. Once we know for sure, we can decide what to do next."

Brianne stepped away from Alex and hugged her torso. "You can do it without me."

"Maybe. But we both knew Carter, and I think it'll be easier —"

"I can't."

"Of course you can."

She shook her head.

Alex didn't want to pressure her, but she couldn't say no. He needed her. "I know it won't be easy, but I'll be there with you every step of the way."

"This is all too much to process right now. I need time. Will you give me that?"

"Of course," he said. "Absolutely. I'll give you my number and you call me whenever."

"I'm not making any promises."

"That's fine." Alex wasn't about to pressure her, even if he needed her. Brianne would want to know. He felt that in his heart. She would think things over and then call him and tell him she wanted to help him find Carter.

At least he hoped so.

Because she had the key to finding Carter.

"I've got a business card in the car. I'll go get it."

Brianne nodded.

Alex went to the front door and jogged down the steps. There was a chill in the November air, reminiscent of the day he and Carter had gone into the mountain three years ago. Three years that had changed his life.

Because Carter hadn't just destroyed him emotionally when he'd disappeared on that mountain. If Alex was right, he had taken the one thing from him more precious than any money.

While he and Carter had been hiking in the Canadian Rockies, someone had ransacked Alex's home, emptying the safe of not only its cash but of a family heirloom that meant the world to him.

On her deathbed, Alex's mother had given him a ring that had once belonged to her mother. His mother had told him that since she hadn't had any daughters, she was passing the antique diamond engagement ring to him. That he should give it to the woman he would ultimately marry.

The memory burned him as he retrieved a business card from his car. At the time, he'd considered it a cruel twist of fate that his home had been robbed at the same time that his friend went missing. Now, he didn't think it a coincidence at all.

His gut told him it was all a part of Carter's plan.

Alex went back to Brianne's front door. She swung the door open before he could.

To his surprise, he saw tears in her eyes.

"Brianne," he said with alarm. "Are you okay?"

She wiped at her eyes and forced a smile. "Yeah, I'm fine. Just overwhelmed, is all."

Guilt slammed into him. Maybe it was unfair to involve her in his plan. She had gone through so much as it was . . .

"I'll be fine," she told him. "You have your card?"

"Yeah," he replied and passed it to her. "The office number is on there, and my cell. You can reach me anytime."

Nodding, she accepted the card. "Okay. I'll call you."

"I'll talk to you later, then," Alex said.

"Mmm hmm."

Again, he was struck by her loveliness, and her vulnerability. His heart quickened.

Ignoring the feeling, he turned away from her and trotted down the steps.

He hoped it wasn't a mistake to involve

46

her in this. And yet, he didn't know of another way.

He had to do what he had to do to get back what was taken from him.

Alex could live without the money that had been stolen from his place. Insurance had replaced it, anyway. But the ring that had meant so much to his mother. That was irreplaceable.

Alex wanted it back. And he intended to get it.

CHAPTER 3

Brianne went to the living room's front window and peered outside. Alex's car was still there, as if he were waiting for something. But moments later, she heard the engine turn over and his sleek and expensive Mercedes drove away from the curb. Only when his car was out of view did she ease back and let her body fall onto the plush sofa.

Carter. Alive. Could it be possible?

Brianne pulled her knees onto the sofa, holding them close to her chest. Her head was spinning. She felt more ambiguous than hopeful, more confused as opposed to certain about what she should do.

Why now? she thought. Why at a point when she had just resolved to let go of any hope that Carter was alive had Alex shown up at her door?

Was this a sign from God? A sign that she should *not* be giving up on Carter?

Brianne sat for several minutes, holding Alex's card in her palm. What had happened was so bizarre that she almost couldn't be sure if she were dreaming.

But she was awake, no doubt about it, which meant that what had just happened had actually happened.

She glanced down at the card in her hand. The name ALEX THORPE was written in big, bold letters. She didn't know what was more unsettling, Alex's sudden appearance at her door or what he'd told her.

Carter. Alive. How long she had waited to hear those words . . . Why wasn't she jumping for joy?

Brianne got up from the sofa and went to her bedroom. Her best friend, Salina, was in New York pursuing her career as a chef and her new man. Brianne called her cell but got no answer. Again. The last she had heard from Salina was two weeks ago, and she'd said that she was working long hours, was stressed but that otherwise all was good.

"Hey, girl," Brianne said when the voice mail picked up. "Something *major* just happened. Call me. I need to talk to someone."

Unable to reach Salina, Brianne went to the closet, retrieved her suitcase and found the travel documents she'd had for her sister's wedding at the Gran Bahia Principe hotel in Jamaica. She didn't like the idea of disturbing Shayna while she was on her honeymoon, but this was an emergency.

She called the hotel in Jamaica. Within minutes, she was connected to her sister's room.

After the third ring, Brianne thought no one was going to answer. Not that she expected them to. Either Shayna and Donovan were out enjoying an evening show at the resort, or they were doing what honeymooners did best. But just before the fourth ring, someone picked up the receiver.

Brianne heard some shuffling, and then, "Hello?"

"Shayna!" Brianne exclaimed, happy to hear her sister's voice. She didn't realize until that exact moment how much she needed her sister right now.

"Brianne?"

"I'm sorry to call you on your honeymoon. I wouldn't have called if it wasn't very, very important." Brianne heard Donovan ask something along the lines of if she was okay. "Yes, tell Donovan I'm okay. Well, actually I'm not too sure that I am."

"What's going on, Bree?" Shayna asked, her voice laced with concern. "Oh, of course. How could I have forgotten? It's today. The three-year anniversary."

"Oh, Shay." A little sob escaped Brianne. "I just talked to Alex, and he said something. Something that's hard to believe."

"Alex? As in Carter's best friend?"

"Yes."

"I thought he'd left Buffalo."

"So did I. But apparently he's back."

"He just called out of the blue?"

"He came to the house."

"Oh, God." Shayna's voice was barely a whisper, and Brianne knew her sister was coming to the same conclusion she had. "They found Carter's remains."

"That's what I thought, too, when I saw him. But Shay, he said something that has me reeling. He thinks . . ." Brianne paused, inhaled deeply. "He thinks that Carter's *alive.*"

"What? How?"

Brianne took the next few minutes to fill her sister in, tell her everything Alex had said. "He wants me to go to Florida to help find Carter. But I don't think I can. I mean, what if it was just a look-alike Alex saw? It's been so hard for me already, trying to deal with the unrealistic likelihood that Carter might come back one day. In so many ways, it might have been easier if I'd just accepted that he had died. So what if we get to Florida and find this person and it's *not*

Carter after all? I don't know if I can deal with that."

"I don't even know what to say, sis. I'm totally in shock."

Again, Brianne heard Donovan speaking, and then she heard Shayna's muffled voice as she filled her husband in on what was happening.

"A part of me is too scared to hope," Brianne said. "But what if Carter *is* alive and he needs me? Or what if he's alive and he's got this whole new life that I won't fit into?"

"I'd want to know," Shayna said. "If you go and learn that it was simply a Carter look-alike, that'll probably help you with closure. You can probably put to bed the idea of Carter ever coming back. But if you go and discover that against all odds Carter is alive . . . Yes, it would be hard to find out that he was involved with someone else, but will it be any easier wondering?"

Shayna had a good point. "Not really. No. It's the wondering that has been so hard these past years."

"Then again, Alex could deal with this on his own and report back to you what he finds. Especially if he learns that Carter has a wife and kids."

A wife and kids. The words made a lump

form in Brianne's throat. She always thought that she would be Carter's wife and the mother of his children.

"I'm sorry," Shayna said. "I shouldn't have said that."

"No, don't apologize. Nothing about this situation is sweet and rosy. I have to accept that."

A beat passed, then Shayna asked, "What do you want to do?"

"I don't know. That's why I called you. To get your input."

"Truthfully, I think that Alex probably saw a guy who looked a lot like Carter, but I doubt it was him. If Carter were alive, then he would have needed medical attention at some point. The authorities would certainly have been called. Then there's the issue of him coming back to America without his identification. Brianne, I can't see this person truly being him."

"But there was no body." Brianne spoke the words more to herself, thinking about the amount of times she had refused to believe Carter dead simply because his jacket and backpack had been found.

"I know," Shayna agreed. "But you know what the authorities think. And there was enough blood on the jacket that they believed there had to have been some sort of attack."

"Yes, yes, I know." Brianne sighed. "Sorry, Shay. I'm not trying to be testy. It's just . . . I still can't think about what might have happened to Carter. It's too hard."

"Brianne, you have to decide what's best for you to do. If you think going to Florida will help, then go. But if it's going to be more painful than anything, then I think you shouldn't do it."

"I thought you said you'd want to know."

"I did, yes. But when I really think about it, the likelihood of it — and how your emotions will get dragged through the ringer again — I don't think it's worth it. That said, I'll support whatever decision you make."

"I know you will," Brianne said softly. "Thanks for listening. I'm sorry I disturbed you."

"Are you kidding? I'm glad you called. I'm just sorry that you're there by yourself dealing with this."

"Tell Donovan hi. I'm gonna let you go."

"All right. But, Bree, if you need to talk again, don't hesitate to call back."

Brianne heard the note of concern in Shayna's voice and loved her sister for it. If not for Shayna, Brianne might not have

54

come out of the dark days of depression after Carter's disappearance.

"Go back to whatever it is you two love-birds were doing," Brianne said, injecting humor into her voice. "I'll see you when you get back."

"Take care, sis. I love you."

"I love you, too," Brianne said.

Brianne ended the call and sat in the dark room, her thoughts once again going back to Carter. More specifically, to the day she had learned from Alex that Carter hadn't come off of the mountain.

Never in her life had she gone through a more emotionally wrenching time. For a twenty-four-year-old, deeply in love and losing the man she adored — it had been too much to bear.

Of course, she'd been devastated. But she'd been most upset with the searchers and the authorities and everyone who had been willing to write Carter off as dead. Determined to prove them all wrong, she had booked a ticket to head to British Columbia and search the mountain herself if necessary. Her sister had gone with her for support. But while in Canada, Brianne had realized how utterly helpless she was to effect any change. The amount of snow was unbelievable, and she — a woman who couldn't stand a day of camping in decent weather — was never going to be able to find Carter when the search team couldn't.

Once the search had been called off and she'd returned home, Brianne had gone into a depression. She had stayed in bed, not eating, not drinking. But her family had been there for her, bringing her plates of food and hot tea. Brianne refused it all until she could no longer starve herself. Then she'd fed her turbulent emotions with food. Within six months, she'd put on the thirty pounds she had spent the year and a half with Carter working off.

She knew how she got when it came to her emotions — unable to truly control them and helpless to assuage herself. It was the reason that going to Florida was such a daunting idea for her. If her hopes were once again deflated . . .

"Sleep on it," Brianne said softly to herself. "And pray on it. When you wake up, you'll know what to do."

She settled in her bed with the rough draft of the novel her sister had just finished. Brianne always read Shayna's books to give her input before she submitted them to her editor. But despite her sister's compelling writing, Brianne simply couldn't lose herself in the fictional historical world.

I think you were right all along. I think Carter's alive.

Instead of concentrating on the words her sister had written, Brianne kept hearing Alex's words. Kept seeing the serious look on his face. And something suddenly struck her about the visit, something that she hadn't picked up on before.

Alex had relayed the news about Carter likely being alive, but he hadn't seemed happy. He hadn't seemed excited about the idea of reconnecting with his best friend.

The realization made her feel better. Because she herself wasn't jumping up and down for joy — something she'd always expected she would do if she'd ever learned that Carter was alive.

Maybe it was all just too surreal to truly accept, given that three years had passed. And they really didn't know for sure. What point was there in getting all excited, only to learn that this was all a mistake?

Of course both she and Alex were guarded. It only made sense that they keep an emotional guard up until they learned the truth.

"Lord, help me deal with this," Brianne whispered. "If Carter's alive, help me truly deal with all of what's to come."

You could want something so badly, yet

57

when it happened you were unprepared for it.

Brianne lowered the manuscript pages. That was also it, she realized. Not just the uncertainty of not knowing if Alex was right about having seen Carter, but the reality that she was unprepared for the unexpected news Alex had delivered — no matter how much she had wished for it. In the early months or even after the first year, had Alex told her that he suspected Carter was alive, she would have been elated. Now, with the amount of time that had passed, there was so much to consider in the event that Carter had somehow escaped death. Because she was not foolish enough to believe that she was just going to pick up the pieces with him and everything would easily go back to the way it was.

She looked at her bedside phone, then at the card Alex had given her that rested on the table beside the phone. She wanted to call Alex now, to confide in him her fears. To talk candidly about the ambiguity she was feeling. She sensed that Alex would tell her that he had his own reservations about how all of this would play out.

Of course, it was different for him. He had been Carter's friend. That was different than being a lover. He could easily pick up and continue as Carter's friend in a way she wasn't sure she would be able to easily continue on as the special woman in his life.

She picked up the card, stared at the phone number. And then she lifted the receiver.

But just as quickly she returned the receiver to its cradle. What was she going to say to him? Ask him all the same questions she had asked him earlier?

There was a part of her that simply wanted to hear his voice, to know that today hadn't been a dream. But it was after nine. She didn't want to disturb Alex.

After all, what if he weren't alone?

An odd twinge came with the thought. In all the time she'd known him, she hadn't known him to have a serious girlfriend. Carter had said that Alex was the consummate playboy. Gorgeous. Rich. He could have his pick of women, and, from what Carter had said, tended to like models.

Brianne was the exact opposite of his type. She was five-foot-five and voluptuous, with curves she had to work to keep in a nice proportion. Not tall and thin.

Not that it mattered. Why was she even thinking about that?

What mattered now was not getting Alex's hopes up until she made a decision. When she called him, it would be to tell him whether or not she had decided to accompany him to Florida.

If you think going to Florida will help, then go. But if it's going to be more painful than anything, then I think you shouldn't do it.

Remembering Shayna's words gave Brianne a sense of comfort. Her sister was right. She didn't have to do anything she didn't want to do — especially if it was painful.

And Brianne didn't know if she could handle seeing Carter if he didn't remember her.

Worse, she didn't know if she could handle seeing him if he were involved with someone else.

The next morning, Brianne's ambiguity over what to do made her angry with herself. She had been sitting at her desk, researching possible causes for temporary amnesia via the internet, and now pushed her chair back and stood. Why was she afraid to deal with a challenging situation? She had been ready to walk down the aisle with Carter, and in her vows she would have promised to be there for her husband in good times and bad. Sure, they hadn't actually gotten married — because fate had intervened. What would she have done if she'd been married to Carter and *then* he'd disappeared? Bailed on him when he needed help?

Brianne made her way downstairs. She needed coffee. *If Carter is alive, how can I not go to him?* she asked herself as she descended the steps. *No matter how hard it might be, how can I not help him get back to his former self?*

Brianne set the Irish cream–flavored coffee to brew, then went back to her bedroom. There she reached for a stuffed teddy bear on her dresser, one she'd had from childhood. She held the bear close to her chest, drawing comfort from her childhood toy. Carter had always teased her for still having a teddy bear she turned to for comfort, but old habits die hard.

Her heart rate accelerated. Was it possible that Carter truly was alive?

The thought was overwhelming. And she needed to talk to someone about it. There was one only one person who understood what she was going through because he himself had experienced it — and that was Alex.

Brianne moved to her night table and lifted the card he'd given her. Then she plopped down on her bed and lifted the receiver.

She dialed the cell number, which rang four times before going to voice mail. Only then did she consider that at only ten minutes after eight, Alex might still be in bed.

Brianne hung up, not wanting to leave a message.

She was surprised when, not more than ten minutes later, the phone rang in the kitchen — and the caller ID showed Alex's number.

CHAPTER 4

"Hello?" Brianne said.

"You called me?" came the deep reply.

She'd already known it was Alex calling her, and yet her stomach fluttered at the sound of his voice. Obviously she was anxious over everything.

"Yeah," she said softly. "I'm sorry. I hope I didn't wake you."

"I've been up since six-thirty. I went to the gym, then came home and was in the shower when you called."

Wow. Talk about dedication. Not that she was surprised. His body was still amazing.

"Oh. Well, that's good then."

"Have you made a decision?" Alex asked.

"I don't know," she admitted. "I wanted to talk more than anything else."

"What's on your mind?"

She hesitated. "Do you feel . . ."

"Feel what?"

Brianne suddenly wasn't sure how to pose

the question.

"Brianne?" Alex prompted.

"Ambiguous," she said, forcing the word from her throat. "A little uncertain about everything?"

"Of course I do," Alex said. "Brianne, I know this isn't going to be easy."

"It's just . . . I want to be there for Carter. If I were the one lost out there somewhere, I'd want him to try to find me. And yet . . ."

On the other end of the line, Alex's breath caught in his chest. "Yet your feelings aren't the same?" he suggested.

A few seconds passed — seconds in which Alex didn't breath. Then Brianne said the words that burst his bubble of hope.

"No, it's not that my feelings have changed. It's that I'm scared."

Alex was angry with himself. Angry that even for a smidgen of a second he had entertained the idea that Brianne was over Carter. A full year after Carter's disappearance, Brianne had been hanging on to the hope that he would return. Three years later, she was still single. Obviously she was still in love with him — even if he was unworthy of that love.

"I know you're scared," Alex said. "I am, too. I mean, we don't know what we're dealing with."

"Exactly," Brianne said softly. "Maybe the unknown is better."

"Really?" Alex asked.

"No. Not really." Brianne blew out a huff of air. "Those are my nerves talking."

"You want to get together for breakfast or something?" Alex suggested. "I've got to be at the store at ten, but we can meet quickly if you want."

"No, I didn't want to disturb you."

"You're not disturbing me."

"It's just . . . I think I need a bit more time to decide what I'm going to do."

"And you don't want me pressuring you until you've made your decision."

"No, no. It's not that." Alex heard a sigh. "You must think me crazy."

"Brianne, I'm the one who showed up at your door after us not talking for two years, and then I dropped a bombshell. Needing time to think things over is not crazy."

"Thank you," she said. And then, "I'm going to get something to eat myself. I'll talk to you later, okay?"

"Sure." Alex spoke calmly. But as he replaced the receiver, anxiety gripped his gut.

He needed Brianne to go with him to Florida.

It was the only way.

Brianne hadn't planned on it, but she left her house two hours before she was scheduled to go to work and drove to Outdoor Gear, located in downtown Buffalo on Broadway. The store was close to the 33 Expressway, which would lead her right to the mall.

She had made her decision. If the amount of time she'd spent thinking about Carter since last night was any indication, she wouldn't be at peace until she knew one way or another.

Still, as Brianne approached the store, she had a sense of unease. But she knew the unease wouldn't dissipate by ignoring the situation.

Brianne slowed and signaled her intent to turn left. She looked out her driver's-side window at the storefront for Outdoor Gear. In three years, she had not come to the sporting goods store that Carter and Alex had bought and run together. She hadn't been able to, knowing that Carter would likely never make another appearance here.

So much had changed in twenty-four hours.

Just as it had changed in an instant three years earlier.

She turned left into the small parking lot, her pulse picking up speed as she parked her car beside Alex's Mercedes. In a flash, she remembered Carter's sleek, 7-series navy blue BMW that used to always be parked back here. Carter and Alex had enjoyed some good-humored bantering over which luxury car was truly the top of the line. Alex believed, hands down, that Mercedes made a better car. Carter argued that Mercedes were for old people and that BMWs were the perfect car for a hip, young male.

Brianne actually smiled as she remembered their ribbing and how they'd often gotten her involved to solve the dispute. Brianne had always sided with her man — though she'd secretly preferred the look of the Mercedes.

The happy memory came and went quickly as she exited her Ford Focus and walked to the store's entrance. She felt oddly nervous. But why should she feel nervous? So what if she hadn't been here in years?

It was like leaving a school and going back to visit. It always felt a little weird. Like you didn't quite belong.

Brianne pulled open the front door, and the door chimes sang. There were a few customers in the store, and Alex was currently speaking with a man near the hockey equipment.

He saw her, and for the briefest of moments their eyes held. Then Brianne jerked her gaze away.

She was suddenly remembering the first time she'd entered this store four and a half years ago. It had been her goal at the time to get into better shape, to begin an exercise routine that consisted of walking and biking.

Alex had been the first one to catch her eye. And he'd smiled, bright and warm. But then Carter had appeared from somewhere off to her right, approaching her before Alex could.

And the rest was history.

Brianne glanced in Alex's direction again. As though he sensed her gaze, he looked at her.

Brianne's stomach fluttered, surprising her.

Obviously she had *not* just felt a zap of attraction for Alex.

It was remembering the first time she'd been in this store and had met Carter. The memory of that day was playing havoc with her emotions.

She perused the store as if she were shopping for something, and when Alex was finally free, he came toward her.

"Hey, Brianne."

"I'll do it," she began without preamble. "I'll work with you to help find Carter."

Alex hesitated a moment, then said, "If you need more time to make your decision —"

"I don't need more time," Brianne interjected. "It was the only decision I could make. Because if Carter's alive, he's obviously suffered some trauma." She paused. "We were engaged. I was months away from marrying him. About to take vows to love him and be there for him forever. So I . . . I have to be there for him now."

"I'm glad," Alex said.

Brianne noticed — not for the first time — just how attractive he was. At six foot four, she had always loved his height. She wondered if he were still single — if Carter's disappearance had him stuck in the past, unable to move forward as she had been.

"So," she began, and sighed. "What do we do next?"

"I say we head to Daytona and hit the ground running. It makes sense to head to the place where I saw him."

"But he could be anywhere now. He could

69

have been visiting Daytona for the event."

"True," Alex acknowledged. "But it seems like the best place to start. We can hit the racing circuit. We can also bring pics of Carter and ask if Dean knows him by another name."

Brianne nodded. "Okay."

"I think the sooner we leave, the better."

"Yeah, that makes sense. I'll have to talk to my district manager, clear the time off with her."

"Oh," Alex said, his tone making it clear he hadn't considered her work might be an issue. "So you might not be able to go —"

"I don't anticipate a problem," Brianne said. "My manager and I get along well. I head in to work shortly, so I'll talk to her then. How long do you think we'll need to be gone?"

"Hard to say. A few days. Maybe a week."

"A week?"

"I don't imagine it'll take longer than that. But what if we get a lead that takes us to another part of the country?"

"Oh." Brianne frowned. "I didn't consider that."

"I'll cover all of your expenses," Alex said. "Your airfare, hotel. And if losing the time from work is going to be a financial burden, I can help you out there, too. In fact, consider it done."

"You don't need to do that," Brianne said.

"Yeah, I do. I'm the one dragging you into this with me. Besides, business is going well."

Brianne didn't doubt that. Glancing around the store, she could see that it had been recently renovated. "So you opened a store in Phoenix?"

"Yep."

"Business is going well there?"

Alex nodded. "Yeah. The store's bigger than this one, and it's been busy ever since I opened it."

"How many stores do you have now?"

"Six and counting," Alex answered. "I've even had an offer to open a store abroad."

"Abroad. Wow. Where?"

"In Italy."

So life had been good for him since Carter had disappeared. Brianne didn't know why that surprised her. Life had to go on for those Carter had left behind.

"When do you think you'll be able to get the time off work?" Alex asked. "Ideally, I'd like to leave as soon as possible."

"I'll let you know in a few hours. I'll tell my manager that it's an emergency, and hopefully I'll be ready to leave by tomorrow. Sound good?"

"Sounds good."

"All right, then." Brianne began to walk to the door, and Alex fell into step beside her. "I'll talk to you later."

"Later, Brianne."

It didn't take Brianne long to get things straightened out at work. As soon as she called the district manager and told her what was going on, Marlene okayed her request for further time off.

Brianne waited until her break to call Alex.

"Brianne?" he said the moment he answered his cell.

"It's a go," she told him. "My district manager has agreed to give me a week off, starting tomorrow."

"Great," Alex said, and Brianne could tell he was smiling.

"I can't believe we're really doing this, that this is really happening," Brianne said.

"I know what you mean," Alex agreed. "But hopefully before next week rolls around, we'll have found Carter."

Brianne inhaled a shaky breath, thinking about Alex's words.

Would everything work out the way they hoped?

Next week this time, would she be reunited with her long-lost fiancé?

CHAPTER 5

Alex heard his iPhone sing and thought he was dreaming.

But a moment later he realized that his phone was indeed ringing.

Groggy, he glanced at the clock and saw that it was shortly after one in the morning. Then he reached for his singing phone.

Seeing Brianne's number, he was instantly alarmed. Why was she calling him at this hour?

"Brianne?" he said cautiously. "Is that you?"

"I'm sorry to call, and so late, but no one's here, and — and I'm scared —"

Alex bolted upright, his alarm intensifying. "Whoa, Brianne. Why are you scared? What's going on?"

"There's a big ruckus outside. Sounds like someone's fighting right outside my door."

"Have you gone to the door?"

"No. I'm afraid to even look out the window."

"Good. Stay inside."

"There have been problems with the people next door. They bought a house that was in foreclosure, and I think the old owners have been harassing them. I don't want to be paranoid, but I'm the only one here, and what if someone pulls out a gun?"

"It doesn't sound like you're paranoid. I'm on my way."

"No, I don't think that's a good idea," Brianne said. "I don't even know why I called you. I should just call the police."

"It won't take me too long to get there," Alex said, out of bed and already reaching for his jeans. "I'll drive by, see what's happening. But if the disturbance continues, don't hesitate to call the cops. I don't want a stray bullet going into your place."

"Okay," Brianne said, her voice shaky.

Moments after Alex disconnected with Brianne, he was dressed and heading down the stairs in his home. He ran out the back door off the kitchen and charged toward his car. Within seconds, he was speeding to Brianne's house.

He saw the police cruiser the moment he turned onto her street. His heart rate sped up as he wondered if he was too late, if

74

something had happened in the ten minutes since Brianne had called him.

But as he drove nearer to Brianne's house, he saw a young couple, both wearing robes, standing near the sidewalk while talking to two police officers. Alex narrowed his eyes, wondering what was going on. That's when he noticed the white picket fence had been vandalized — likely kicked viciously until it had been mostly broken. Not just the fence, he noticed. There was a huge hole in the house's front window.

Someone had hurled a rock through it.

He parked several feet past Brianne's house to keep out of the way of the police. As he walked back to Brianne's place, his eyes landed on the car in the driveway next to her house. It, too, had been vandalized. It had been kicked and keyed, and one of the side windows smashed to pieces.

Talk about overkill.

The couple and the officers both looked in Alex's direction. It was late, and he didn't want to appear suspicious. So before he made his way up the walkway to Brianne's house, he said without preamble, "My friend who lives here called me. She was scared because of the commotion. I said I'd drop by, check in on her."

The taller officer nodded, giving Alex no

trouble. Alex knew he wasn't on the cops' radar. Given what Brianne had said, it had to be the former occupants who had lost their home who were behind the late-night vandalism.

Alex hopped up the steps and knocked on the door. Within two seconds, it opened. Brianne stood there in pink flannel pajamas, looking up at him with a worried expression.

"You shouldn't have just opened the door like that," Alex said.

"I knew it was you," Brianne explained. "I saw your car pull up. Plus, the cops are outside. I knew it was safe now." She stepped backward, pulling the door fully open.

Alex stepped into the foyer. "Are you okay?"

Brianne nodded her head jerkily. "Yeah."

Alex didn't think, just drew Brianne into his arms and held her, offering comfort.

"I feel a little bit silly," she said after a moment. "I shouldn't have called you. The cops are here, and I'm fine. It's just —"

"Don't apologize. I'm glad you called." Alex released her and eased back. "So, what's the story next door?"

"It's a sad story, really," Brianne said. "The people who used to live next door lost their house when the economy went down-hill. Of course, the bank then sold the house for a lot less. It's so unfair. You take the house from people who have put blood, sweat and tears into it, and then you sell it to someone else for a steal."

"You feel sorry for the former owners?" Alex asked disbelievingly. "Even after what they did?"

"I feel sorry for what they went through, but I don't condone what they've done. I mean, I understand the former owners' frustration, but to take it out on the new owners? That's not fair. Not to mention that vandalizing property and disturbing the rest of us is definitely not fair."

"You sure that it's the former owners?"

"I think so. We all do. That house is the only one that has been vandalized. Rocks thrown through the windows, the siding spray painted. Now the fence and the car."

"If you're right, then the former owners are really stupid. They'd have to know that this would come back to them."

"I don't think it's the actual owners," Brianne explained.

Alex frowned. "You've lost me."

"I mean, I don't think either of the parents are responsible for the vandalism. But they had a teenaged son and daughter who took the move badly, from what I understand. It's got to be one of them." Brianne hugged her torso. "I'm kind of glad I'm heading to Florida with you. I have a feeling the situation is going to escalate, and I really don't want to be here for that. It's bad enough being here in the house by myself."

Alex didn't plan to suggest this, the words just came from his mouth. "Why don't you get your luggage and come with me?"

Brianne's eyes widened in surprise. "You want me to go to your place?"

"We leave late tomorrow morning, anyway. This saves me making another trip here to pick you up. Are you packed for Florida?"

"Yes, but —"

"No buts. I've got more than enough room. And if you're worried about me getting in your way, don't. You can have a floor all to yourself."

"You getting in *my* way?" Brianne asked, regarding him with wide eyes. "It's your house. And I don't want to impose." Wait a minute . . . had he just said she could have a *floor* all to herself?

"Humor me."

"Alex, it's not really necessary."

"When I was in college, someone I knew was going through something similar to this. Neighbors who were a problem. That girl ended up in the middle of a dispute that had nothing to do with her. She got stabbed. I don't want to take any chances with you."

Brianne couldn't argue with his logic. Bad things happened to good people all the time. People who were in places they were supposed to be, but at the wrong time.

Besides, she could tell by the look on Alex's face that he wasn't going to take no for an answer.

Alex strolled toward the opening to the living room. "I'll wait here while you get changed."

"Okay," Brianne said, not bothering to protest. And there was something about the fact that Alex wanted to protect her that made her feel a warm tingle. Again, she found the reaction odd. But once again, she dismissed it as misplaced. Especially right now, given that he was acting in the role of protector. It was easy to feel a sense of *something* toward him.

Gratitude. That had to be it. He was about to hopefully reunite her with the love of her life. Of course she would feel a sense of gratitude.

But as Brianne made her way up the stairs, she couldn't help thinking that it wasn't gratitude but something else.

■ ■ ■ ■

Half an hour later, Alex was in a neighborhood in Buffalo that Brianne had never been in. A neighborhood with massive houses on large lots.

When Alex slowed and turned into a driveway of one of the larger houses, Brianne's lips parted in surprise. It was an older home with a large wraparound porch, a pool to the left surrounded by a fence and a long driveway. Alex drove to the back of the driveway, where — to Brianne's surprise — she saw another house that was definitely bigger than her parents' home.

"Both of these are your houses?" Brianne asked, knowing she sounded astonished.

"This house back here is a carriage house. It's perfectly fine as a stand-alone house, but I guess it was built for staff, or as an in-law suite."

"In-law suite? It looks much bigger than your average house."

"Three thousand square feet."

"Oh, my," Brianne said, nearly choking. That was nearly twice the size of her parents' home. "What do you do with it?"

"I'm renting it out to a husband and wife. A yuppie couple with no kids who are quite happy here. At least for now."

"Wow. I've never seen a carriage house, except on television. And your house —" She turned to gaze at it from the passenger seat. "It looks massive."

"Sixty-five hundred square feet."

Sixty-five hundred square feet. The words echoed in Brianne's mind. She could hardly believe it.

"May as well leave your suitcase in the car," Alex said. "Unless you've got toiletries in there that you need."

"Actually, I took my toiletries bag out of the suitcase already." She patted the large purse on her lap. "Before we head to the airport, I'll put it back in."

Brianne got out of the car and followed Alex to the back door of the house. It was late, and she had planned to go straight to bed, given that they had to catch a flight in the morning, but the moment she stepped inside she found herself saying, "Can I get the grand tour?" Then, "Actually, it doesn't have to be tonight. I can see the place in the morning."

"If you want the tour, I'll give you the tour."

The first floor was massive — with a giant living room, an equally large kitchen that had been recently remodeled, a dining room and two sitting rooms. It was one of those beautiful old homes that had been immaculately maintained.

Six large bedrooms — seven, if you counted the home gym. Four full bathrooms. Three half baths. Brianne toured it all with open-mouthed wonder.

"And you live here by yourself?" Brianne asked as Alex completed the tour of the fourth level.

"Yeah."

Stepping out of the last, extremely large bedroom that had been converted into a home gym, Brianne faced Alex. "You don't ever get lonely?"

"Sometimes, but after a long day working, I need a place I can come and relax. Totally unwind."

"Well, the place is magnificent," Brianne said as she strolled toward the landing. She reached out and touched the wall, which was painted a pale peach color. She gazed at the African paintings lining the wall going down the stairs. "How long have you owned this place?"

"About a year and a half."

"Did you paint the walls? Or were they like this when you got here?" Brianne had noticed that all the walls had been painted, some pale yellow, some pale peach and some white.

"It was like this."

"Hmm."

"What does that mean? You don't like it?"

Brianne continued a slow walk down the steps, eyeing every detail as she rounded the corner down the landing. "It's perfectly fine."

"But?" Alex asked. "Because I sense one."

Brianne faced him. "It's just . . . a house like this with so much character, and its age . . . I see it with wallpaper. Nothing overbearing. No flowers or fruits. But something sophisticated, like stripes." She ran her hand over the wall. "This one here would look fabulous with a blue-and-white-striped wallpaper." She shrugged. "I don't know. The walls as they are . . . well, they're kinda —"

"Boring?" Alex supplied.

Brianne faced Alex, about to lie, but instead she smiled. "You said it, not me."

"I like the suggestion. I always felt the place was missing something. I figured a woman would put her special touch on it."

"A woman?" Brianne asked, her heart speeding up as she did. "You — you're dating?"

"No." Alex shook his head. "I meant eventually."

"Ah." Brianne nodded, then continued down the stairs to the main level, in a way running from her own emotion. Why on earth would it bother her if Alex were dating?

Her head down, she examined the hardwood floors. They were dark and shiny, but they didn't look new. She figured the former owners had refinished them.

"You don't like the floors?" Alex asked.

"Sorry," Brianne said, waving off the comment. "I didn't mean to come in here and scrutinize the place."

"Which means you don't like the floors."

"I love the floors."

"Phew, I'm relieved. It was a lot of hard work ripping out the carpet and refinishing the original hardwood."

"You did the work?" Brianne asked.

"Don't look so surprised."

"I'm impressed."

"I did have some help. But I put a lot of sweat equity into this place. I figure if I ever sell it —"

"No, don't sell it. It's a perfect house."

"I'm glad you like it."

"The wicker furniture is okay," Brianne said tentatively as she walked into the sitting area near the front door. "But this area would really come alive with some French provincial furniture. And again, I'd add some wallpaper in here. Something delicate. Warm colors."

"Is my design taste that bad? Or do you give this kind of advice to everyone you visit?"

"I'm sorry," Brianne said. "I guess I've watched one too many home decorating shows."

"Ah, so you're into home decorating."

"I wouldn't say I'm *into* it," Brianne clarified. "But when I see a space, I try to imagine how I can improve it."

"You seem to be good at it. Is it something you've considered as a job?"

"No," she answered quickly. Perhaps too quickly, because Alex eyed her skeptically.

"You sure about that?" he asked.

"It was a thought I had. Once. A crazy dream that maybe I could make a career at interior design. Carter brought me back down to earth."

"Whoa — are you saying you talked about your dream with Carter and he talked you out of it?"

"He just pointed out that it's not easy to start a business, and I'd have to spend a lot of time researching and promoting. Not to mention the start-up costs and the endless hours I'd have to put into the job. I think

Carter didn't want me to get caught up in a job that would keep me from being the kind of wife and mother who spends a lot of time at home. He never really said it, but I got the sense that he wasn't close to his mother because of the fact that she was always traveling for work." She shrugged. "I don't know."

"From what I can tell in the short time since you've been here, you have a knack for this. And when people have a knack for something, they should go for it."

"Really, it's more of a hobby," Brianne said. She didn't hold any illusions that she could make a career out of interior design.

"Some hobbies turn into the best careers, because you're doing what you love."

"And some hobbies are meant to be just that."

"Don't say that. I loved sports and adventure. It's why I started Outdoor Gear. Same for Carter. I'm really surprised that he tried to steer you from your dream."

Brianne had thought the same thing at the time, that if anyone should have understood her passion it was Carter. But she also knew how important it was to Carter to marry a woman who would stay at home and raise the children, since he would be providing for her.

She didn't like the memory, so she changed the subject. "I didn't expect you to live in a place like this."

"What kind of place did you expect me to live in?"

"I guess I figured you'd live in the typical bachelor pad, not something with character like this. The condo on the water. Black leather sofas. Maybe a pool table in one of the bedrooms. A revolving door to keep the women coming and going."

"Ouch."

"Sorry . . . I shouldn't have said that."

"Why did you?" Alex asked, giving her a pointed look.

Brianne withered under Alex's gaze. She wished now that she had kept her thoughts to herself. Because she could tell that Alex wasn't going to drop the matter until she answered his question.

"It's just that . . . Carter always talked about how you liked to date a lot of women but would never settle down."

"*Carter* said that?"

"He said that's why you liked dating models. Because they were always traveling and wouldn't be around to suffocate you."

"Wow." Alex planted his hands on his hips.

"Come on," Brianne said, keeping her tone light. "Did you or did you not have a thing for models?"

Alex was inwardly seething, but tried not to show it. "I did date one model," he admitted. But not for the shallow reason Carter had told Brianne. "Actually, two."

"See?" Brianne said.

What he saw was that for some reason, Carter had seen fit to bash him to Brianne. Why? Had Carter suspected that Brianne had been attracted to him?

"You realize the place you described seeing me in is the kind of place Carter had."

Brianne's eyes flew to his. And Alex instantly realized how his words must have sounded.

"No, I don't mean that way. Not the revolving door part. But the bachelor pad bit."

"I know." Brianne smiled, but it was a sad smile. "Carter always said that I was the one woman who was able to lure him from his bachelor ways."

Alex turned, neither agreeing nor disagreeing. Carter had lied to Brianne about who he was. He'd had her fooled and enjoyed that he had so easily been able to manipulate her.

Why had Alex never suspected that he had lied to *him?*

Alex turned back toward Brianne, saw the

expression on her face. Within seconds, it had gone from nostalgia to grim.

"Hey, we're going to find him," Alex said, stepping toward her. He placed a hand on her shoulder.

Brianne looked up at him and smiled softly. "Don't mind me," she said. "I'm just . . . it's tough dealing with this news. Yes, I'm hopeful, but I'm all emotional, too. I never thought I'd ever hear you say that we were going to find Carter. Yet here you are, saying exactly that."

"I mean it, Brianne. We *will* find him."

Brianne stepped backward, away from Alex's touch, even though she knew it had been meant only to comfort. But she was suddenly all too aware of his presence, and the fact that they were alone and the master bedroom was one floor up.

"I'm tired," she announced. "We should be getting to bed."

Something passed over Alex's face, an expression Brianne couldn't read.

"Yeah, you're right." He paused briefly. "I'll show you to your room. Because in nine hours, we're going to be on a flight to Florida. One that is hopefully going to change everything."

CHAPTER 6

Brianne had never flown first class before, but she had a feeling she could easily get used to it.

"You mean the drinks are free?" she whispered to Alex once they were airborne.

"I wouldn't exactly say free, since you certainly pay for them in the price of the ticket. But yes, you can have as many as you want."

Brianne ordered an orange juice mixed with vodka, just so she could have the experience of a "free" drink on a plane. Besides, a drink might help to calm her nerves. They were frayed, given the uncertainty of what would come next.

The oversize leather seat was a luxury she had never experienced on a plane, and she enjoyed pushing it back as far as it could go, knowing that the person behind her wasn't going to groan and give her dirty looks.

Brianne was glad that she'd brought a novel with her, because for the first part of the flight Alex wasn't talkative. He had drifted in and out of slumber ever since they'd gotten on the plane. Brianne suspected he hadn't gotten much sleep.

She hadn't either. She had been far too anxious about this trip to relax and get any rest.

She ordered another drink, read her novel and kept surreptitiously looking at Alex. After about an hour, he suddenly opened his eyes and faced her.

"Hey," Brianne said.

"Was I sleeping?" Alex asked.

"Uh-huh."

Alex leaned forward, stretched. Brianne's eyes followed the movement of the perfectly sculpted muscles of his upper back and arms. He was seriously fine.

She sipped more of her drink.

After a moment she faced Alex again. "Here are your pretzels." She passed the small packet to him. "The flight attendant came by while you were snoozing. And here's your water."

Alex took the water bottle she offered him. "Thanks."

As Alex began to unscrew the bottle cap, Brianne spoke. "I think I know what may have happened to him."

He shot her a quizzical look. "Hmm? You mean to Carter?"

She realized that her words had confused him. "Oh, I don't mean what happened in Florida. I mean what may have happened to him in British Columbia."

Alex sipped his water, and a bead of the liquid clung to his bottom lip. Brianne watched as his tongue flicked out to capture it.

He had full, sexy lips, something she hadn't really noticed before. There were other things she was suddenly taking note of about Alex that she never had. Like the way one cheek dimpled when he smiled. And the small scar beneath his left eye. She wondered if he'd gotten that while doing one sport or other. And then there were his thighs. They were large and strong and looked amazing in a pair of jeans.

Brianne felt a jolt of heat and quickly looked to the left, out the plane window. Why was she suddenly checking Alex out the way she was?

Because she was spending more time with him than she ever had?

"Well, what is it?" Alex asked. "Or are you trying to keep me in suspense?"

Brianne finished the last of her drink

before speaking again, wondering why her pulse was beating at a faster pace. She faced Alex again, saying, "I was looking up various causes of amnesia online, and I stumbled upon a story that really hit me. Have you heard of Lyme disease?"

"I've heard the name. I don't really know anything about it."

"Lyme disease happens when people are bitten by ticks, which usually happens when someone is in the great outdoors. Camping, hiking. The thing is, it's often misdiagnosed, and I read some really fascinating and bizarre cases online. There was one case about a young woman who was bitten, didn't know it and suddenly she started to suffer from amnesia. In a really bad way. She would meet a person and a few minutes later forget who they were."

"Really?"

Brianne nodded, proud of what her research had uncovered, feeling that she could be on to something. She needed to stay focused on the issue at hand, and that issue was finding Carter and getting him the help he needed. Staying focused on Carter would keep her mind from wandering where Alex was concerned.

"Turns out," Brianne went on, "this woman was bitten by a tick and developed

Lyme disease. If treated fairly quickly, antibiotics can correct the condition. But if it isn't treated, people can suffer severely."

"You certainly did a lot of research."

"It's entirely possible that Carter was bitten by a tick and developed Lyme disease. He wouldn't have been treated for it — who would even assume he had it? — and hence he started suffering from the various side effects, amnesia being a big one." Brianne stopped suddenly, realizing that she couldn't read Alex's expression. "You don't think it's possible?"

"Possible, sure. Likely? I don't know."

"But that's the whole point, isn't it? That we don't know. No one wanted to believe me when I said it was possible that Carter was still alive. It was far-fetched, I get it. And yet, here we are. So doesn't it make sense that if he *is* alive, the explanation has to be one that's incredible? Something far out of the realm of normal? If he got off the mountain unharmed, he would have come home. End of story. But if he got off the mountain and *didn't* come home, what could explain that other than something extremely bizarre?"

Alex pressed his lips together, nodded. "I never thought of it that way."

Brianne sensed he wasn't entirely convinced of her theory. "But you agree, don't you? I've got to be right about there being an extremely bizarre explanation as to why he wouldn't have returned home."

"Yeah. If Carter's alive, there's got to be a doozy of an explanation."

Brianne exhaled loudly, butterflies dancing in her stomach. "I'm so nervous, Alex. In my heart, I always knew this day would come, but now that it's here, it's like a dream."

"You've really come around," Alex said.

"What do you mean?"

"Two days ago, when I left your place, I thought I wasn't going to hear from you. I was almost certain you wouldn't want to go with me to Florida. But here you are, all excited."

"It's like you said. If Carter is alive, he needs us. I'm excited, but I'm also scared, too. Especially if Carter has Lyme disease, or amnesia, or heck — what if he's missing a limb? It's scary not knowing what we're in for when we find him."

"One day at a time," Alex said softly. "That's all we can do."

"You're right," Brianne agreed. "We can only cross a bridge when we get to it."

When they landed at the Daytona airport,

Alex led the way to the car rental area as if he'd done it a million times. He didn't stop at the desk, just went straight to a black Lincoln Navigator.

"Don't you have to . . . to sign for it?" Brianne asked.

"I set it all up ahead of time," Alex explained. "They have the car waiting because of the express service I use, which allows me to avoid the hassles of waiting."

"Nice," Brianne said.

Alex retrieved the keys from the visor of the Navigator, then remotely opened the trunk. He loaded the suitcases while Brianne went around to the passenger's seat.

Again, Brianne noted that Alex exited the airport parking lot and seemed to know exactly where he was going, not even consulting the map of Daytona that had been left on the seat.

Brianne took in the scenery as Alex drove. The palm trees. The bright sunshine as opposed to gray skies she had left back in Buffalo. When they passed the Daytona International Speedway, she looked long and hard at the structure, her heart rate increasing. Had Carter truly been there just last month? And if so, how had he arrived in Daytona? How had he gone from lost in the Canadian Rockies to a life in Florida?

Brianne noticed that her hands were shaking and told herself to calm down. So much was riding on this trip, and yet nothing was a given. As hopeful as she was, there was still a part of her that wasn't sure she could truly trust what Alex had said. She had to accept the fact that he could be mistaken about seeing Carter. There were look-alikes all over the world. Maybe Alex had simply seen a dead ringer for Carter.

God, let us find him. Even if the person only turns out to be Carter's look-alike.

The last thing Brianne wanted was to return home with no answers.

If they learned that Alex had actually seen Carter's look-alike, it would be horribly disappointing, but at least they would have an answer. And once and for all, Brianne could accept the fact that Carter was never coming home.

Lost in her thoughts, Brianne was no longer seeing the beautiful Florida scenery. But when she felt the vehicle turn left, she focused on her surroundings again.

They were now in a more populated area. There were a number of hotels and restaurants lining both the left and right sides of the street. As Alex drove past a sprawling Hilton hotel, Brianne glimpsed the stretch of sand and blue water on the right.

"The beach," she said, somewhat excited. "Look at those colors. Beautiful."

"Yeah, this is a really nice spot. Have you ever been to Florida before?"

"Once. To Orlando when I was twelve. The closest beach was an hour away in Tampa, but my family was so busy at Disney and the other theme parks that we never got there."

"You like the beach?"

"What's not to like?"

"Then you'd love Miami. It's far enough south that it's subtropical, so much warmer in the winter even than Daytona. You've got vegetation there that you find in the Caribbean. And the Florida Keys? Now that's a beautiful spot."

"Sounds like you do a lot of traveling."

"A fair bit."

"All for work — or for pleasure?"

"Bit of both."

Alex drove past the last of the hotels — at least the ones that were on the main strip with the others. And when he drove into an area that was clearly residential, Brianne turned to him and narrowed her eyes. "Are you sure we're going the right way? It seems like all the hotels are behind us."

"We're not going to a hotel."

Brianne was sure she must have heard

incorrectly. "Pardon me?"

"We're not going to a hotel."

"I don't understand."

Alex glanced at her and said, "I've got a place down here."

"A place . . . you mean a place you own?"

Alex chuckled softly. "Yeah. A house. It's an investment property."

"Aren't you full of surprises?"

"Does it bother you that we'll be staying at my place?"

Brianne looked to the right, taking in the scenic view of the ocean. She had already stayed at Alex's house in North Buffalo. "No," she replied. "I just didn't expect it."

"Because if you'd feel more comfortable at a hotel . . ."

"We're going to be joined at the hip, anyway," Brianne said, then faced him and smiled, wondering why her heart thundered at her words. "Like I said, I just figured we were going to a hotel. I'm surprised you have a place down here. Is this where you stay in the winter? Or do you have a host of houses all over the world?"

"I have a number of investment properties, and yes, they're in different places around the world."

Brianne had been kidding. "Oh. What kind of places?"

"A villa in Cyprus. Also a place on the outskirts of Rome. A place in Aruba — gorgeous island, if you've never been."

"I haven't," Brianne said softly. "I've always wanted to get to Italy, to see all that wonderful old architecture, the palaces. I've seen them on television and on the internet, but I know that to see it in person would be far more spectacular."

"It is," Alex agreed. "The first time I went to Rome, it took me days to tour the city, and it still didn't feel like I had enough time."

"I'm jealous," Brianne said good-naturedly.

"Don't be. You'll get there one day. Maybe you'll go there for inspiration for one of your wealthy clients."

Brianne narrowed her eyes at him. "What clients?"

"The clients you'll have," Alex said.

Brianne was still confused.

"For your design business."

"Oh," Brianne said, then chuckled. But the chuckle died when she saw that Alex was looking at her with a serious expression.

"Don't laugh, Brianne. I know it's going to happen for you."

There was no question in his statement. He spoke the words as if they were fact. And

Brianne couldn't help smiling softly. She appreciated his confidence in her. Confidence she herself lacked.

"That's a nice dream," she said.

"Every successful business starts as a dream. Dreams become reality, Brianne. You just have to believe that's possible."

Who was this man? Certainly not the Alex Thorpe who had been aloof when she'd been dating Carter.

She had always seen him as distant, and sometimes even a little cold. But in two days, she had gotten to know him on a deeper level and realized that much of what she'd believed about him before simply wasn't true. He wasn't cold and impersonal. He was warm, caring and driven.

He had been Carter's best friend, and he and Brianne had had a cordial relationship, but nothing truly deep. Brianne had always gotten the impression that Alex didn't care much for her, perhaps because she hadn't been the rail-thin model type that men with money tended to date. But he was certainly giving her the moral support she needed to pursue her passion, something Carter had never done.

She was definitely liking the person she was now getting to know.

Brianne eyed the area they were now in.

The houses had gone from being average-size to massive. Neatly trimmed hedges bordered large front lawns. The driveways were long, and some were lined with palm trees. It was the kind of picturesque area Brianne was used to seeing in brochures.

When Alex turned into the circular drive-way of a beige-colored house that had to be at least three times the size of her parents', she actually gasped.

This was Alex's house? His *vacation* house?

The place was like a mini-palace. Unlike his turn-of-the-century Victorian home in Buffalo, this sprawling property looked new, with large bay windows at the front and archways every three feet or so. A myriad of colorful flowers were in the circular base of a palm tree in the middle of the lawn. The lawn's pristine nature told Brianne that someone took care of the property on a regular basis.

"This is your house?" she asked, unable to hide the awe from her voice.

"Yep. My home away from home."

Home away from which home? she wanted to ask, but didn't. Based on the list he had recited to her, he had homes in many places. If he got bored of one place, he could easily pack his things and head to another spot in the world.

"I've never seen anything so big," she said. "And it's right on the beach. This is amazing."

"I like it."

"You said this was an investment property. You rent it out?"

"Yes, a lot of the time I do. I prefer executive rentals, for businessmen who are accustomed to a certain standard of living while away from home. I get some long-term rentals that way."

"But no one's here now," Brianne said, knowing there couldn't be, but wanting to be sure. Not that there wasn't enough room for fifty people in this house . . .

"Not right now. I was planning to come here over the winter, so I didn't rent it out."

"Escape the gray skies and snowstorms in Buffalo. Nice."

"Mmm hmm."

Alex opened his car door first, then Brianne did the same, stepping out onto the interlock stone driveway. Carter hadn't had anything this lavish when he and Brianne had been together. He'd had a magnificent townhouse on the water and a condo in the city, but nothing like this.

Alex got the suitcases from the trunk of the Navigator. Brianne offered to carry one, but he told her he was fine. So she opened the back door of the car and removed her carry-on and purse.

She suddenly wanted to call her sister, tell her where she was. Shayna would no doubt be surprised. Brianne had never left home for a trip on her own.

No, she wasn't alone.

She was with Alex.

Carter's best friend.

Brianne felt a niggle of something. But what? That this was wrong? That she shouldn't be alone in a house with another man?

This isn't a romantic trip, she told herself. *You're here with Alex because you're trying to find Carter. No other reason.*

Maybe what she felt was a tinge of regret. She had always wanted to travel the world, but after Carter had disappeared she hadn't done any traveling. She had let Carter's disappearance hold her back on so many levels. She should have gotten on a plane and gone somewhere — anywhere — but didn't possess the courage to do so alone. She was envious of her sister's ability to do just that earlier this year. Shayna had gone on a solo honeymoon after her marriage to Vince didn't happen. Brianne had been worried about her traveling to Jamaica alone, but in the end, it had been the best trip for Shayna. She'd met Donovan, the man she had just married.

Brianne followed Alex under the archway that led to the front door. She took in her surroundings — the large, neatly trimmed hedge, the thick blades of grass she wasn't used to in Buffalo. All the vibrant colors of the flowers.

The porch was massive, the kind that would be nice to sit on in the morning and drink a cup of tea. She especially liked the porch swing, which gave the place a homey touch.

Then Alex opened the door — and Brianne's mouth fell open.

CHAPTER 7

Good Lord in heaven. This was Alex's home?

The entranceway alone was stunning. Beige-colored marble floors sparkled. A winding staircase led to the second level and a large hallway above. The immediate foyer went from the ground level all the way to the second level. Above them hung a dazzling chandelier, which looked like it was made from hundreds of beads of crystal.

Brianne hadn't known what to expect when Alex had said he was taking her to his vacation home, but she hadn't expected anything like this.

That's not true. She had expected a modest home, close to the beach. The kind that would suffice for a week or two or even a month. But this . . . this was beyond incredible.

She couldn't help wondering what his other properties were like.

Alex led the way upstairs. "There are five bedrooms," he announced. "Four up here, and one downstairs. Other than the master bedroom, which I always use, you can pick any one you want."

"Which one is the master?"

"The one on the right with the double doors." Alex gestured in the direction.

Brianne nodded. She strolled toward the door to her immediate left, certain that the room would be sufficient. She didn't need to examine the other three bedrooms on this floor to determine which would suit her needs for a few days.

She opened the door to the bedroom. She should have been past being surprised at this point, but clearly she wasn't. This bedroom was absolutely huge, with a gorgeous canopy bed in its center. After taking in the impressive bed, her eyes immediately went to the fireplace on the right wall.

And was that . . . ?

Brianne couldn't help feeling giddy as she rushed into the room. Yes, they were doors that led to a terrace. Even before she reached for the door handle, she could see the stretch of beach.

"Are you serious? A view of the beach?"

She tried to open the door but found it locked. She took a few moments to unlock the door and then rushed onto the balcony.

She gasped again. The view of the ocean and stretch of beach was to die for.

So was the view of the kidney-shaped pool below.

Heaven. That's what this place was. She almost wanted to let out a little scream.

Somehow, she kept her emotions in check. And a moment later, she was remembering the reason she was here in this gorgeous place. It was simply the base camp from which they would mount their operation to find Carter.

Brianne turned and faced Alex. She must have been smiling like a fool, because he said, "You like it?"

"Gosh, Alex — what's not to like? I can't . . . I can't believe you have a house like this."

"You could have it, too," he said.

Was Brianne imagining it, or did something just flicker in Alex's eyes? Something she couldn't read. Something that made her skin flush.

"If you pursue your dream," Alex quickly said, as if he realized how his words might have been construed. "When you work for yourself, the sky's the limit."

"I can see that," Brianne said, and once again faced the stunning view of the water.

"Do you have a gym in this house, too?" Brianne asked. Turning back to him, she said, "Not that you need to. You've got the pool. The beach."

"Yeah, I've got a gym. Downstairs."

"Great. I'll make sure to use it — if you don't mind. I don't want to stop my workout routine while I'm away. Can't risk putting on any weight."

"Of course I don't mind. But for what it's worth, you could certainly put on a few pounds and it wouldn't be a big deal." Alex stepped toward her, his gaze traveling over her from head to toe. "You look . . . amazing."

A definite frisson of heat passed through Brianne's body. The compliment had been genuine and heartfelt — and made her feel sexier than she ever had before.

Alex raised his eyes, meeting her gaze. And though Brianne felt the urge to look away, she didn't. She held his gaze, an odd warmth spreading through her.

"But then," he went on, "you always carried your curves well."

"Are you serious?" she asked.

"Absolutely," Alex said. "You've always been beautiful."

Brianne wanted to pinch herself. Alex was telling her that she was beautiful? Hearing

109

it from Alex meant the world, because he was the kind of man women tripped over themselves to get to. "I . . . I don't know what to say."

"Say thank you."

"Thank you."

"You looked stunned," Alex said. "Why?"

"Because . . . because I've never thought I was beautiful," she admitted, not sure why she was sharing the deeply personal thought. "Don't get me wrong. I know I'm cute. Especially now that I've lost weight."

"You've always been beautiful," Alex said, his gaze steady on hers. "Not just now that you're thinner."

Brianne's lips parted. She couldn't believe her ears.

"I always thought you were beautiful the way you were," Alex went on. "You look great now, sure, but I kind of miss those rocking curves."

Brianne couldn't help it — she blushed. She never would have guessed that Alex had liked anything about her. During the time she'd dated Carter, he had always been polite, but he was never warm toward her.

"Great, I've offended you," Alex said. "You know what, forget everything I said other than the 'beautiful' part. I keep forgetting the rule that a man should never comment on a woman's weight."

"Are you kidding? You didn't offend me. You just told me that I'm beautiful at any size. Trust me, those are words a woman loves to hear."

Carter had always been on her to lose about fifteen pounds, at a time when she'd actually been happy with her weight. She wasn't one of those people who wanted to be as thin as a rail. Then Carter had disappeared — and she had drowned her sorrows in food. It was only in preparation for her sister's wedding that she'd started a strict diet and workout regimen again. She had been pleased with the result, but she did miss the sexy curves she used to have. To hear Alex say what he did meant a lot to her.

"Why aren't you married?" she suddenly asked.

"Me?" Alex said, as though she couldn't possibly be talking to him.

Brianne looked around the vast bedroom, then back at him to emphasize her point. "Who else would I be talking to here? Of course I'm referring to you."

Alex shrugged. "Never met the right girl, I guess."

"Or is no one good enough for you?" Brianne suggested.

"Why would you say that?"

"Because even when I was dating Carter, you hardly dated anyone. Correction. You used to *date* a lot, but I don't remember you having one serious girlfriend."

"Because I was breaking every model's heart," Alex said, his voice dripping with sarcasm. "Isn't that what Carter told you?"

"So you admit it?"

Clearly, Brianne had missed his sardonic tone. "No, Brianne. I don't admit that."

"Then why are you single? A gorgeous guy like you, settled in your career. A great catch for any woman."

Alex stepped onto the balcony. He walked to the railing and wrapped his fingers around it as his eyes took in the view of the ocean.

He didn't want to answer this question. Because the answer was one he didn't understand himself. And he certainly couldn't tell Brianne the truth.

And the truth was both complicated and simple. When Alex had met Brianne, he had fallen for her instantly. He didn't know why. It was one of those connections he didn't understand. He'd been drawn to her, then hurt that Carter had made a play for her. That should have been it, but every time he saw her, he felt that undeniable pull of attraction toward her, stronger than anything he had ever known.

Sure, he had dated other women. But he had never again felt that inexplicable pull of attraction for any of those women that he'd felt for Brianne.

Even before he learned the truth about Carter — that his behavior was ultimately going to crush Brianne — he had hoped she would come to her senses and realize that Carter wasn't right for her.

And that *he* was.

Which had been a fantasy at best. Carter had been his best friend, and he never would have dated Brianne if the time ever came that they broke up.

At least not then.

Now was an entirely different matter.

"Did someone break your heart?" Brianne asked. Alex looked to his right and saw her standing there, a vision of loveliness if he'd ever seen one. "Is that why you don't date seriously?"

"I'm not sure why Carter tried to paint me as some major player, but that's not true."

"So you've had some serious girlfriends," Brianne said, her eyes widening slightly. Alex couldn't quite read the emotion in their depths.

"There've been a couple of women I've dated seriously. But why the interest in my love life?"

"How long is serious?" Brianne went on, ignoring the question he'd asked her.

Alex gazed into the distance for a long moment before speaking. "The first one I dated for about five months. That last one . . . off and on for about a year."

"A year. That's a long time."

"I know. Doesn't bode well for my player status. Speaking of which, I don't understand why you and Carter ever spent any time talking about my love life."

Brianne shrugged. "He was worried about you, I guess. He wanted you to find the kind of love he'd found with me."

Alex's fingers tightened on the railing. *More like he wanted to keep you under his clutches.* He couldn't help wondering if Carter had sensed Alex's attraction to Brianne and had taken steps to make sure that she would never be tempted to go for him.

"Who was she?"

Given that he'd been lost in his own thoughts, Alex was temporarily confused by Brianne's question. But catching on, he said, "No one."

"No one?" Brianne eyed him skeptically.

"You dated someone named No One for a year?"

"Brianne, what's with all the questions?"

"I'm just curious."

"Her name is Catarina," Alex answered after a moment.

"Catarina." Brianne rolled the woman's name around on her tongue. "I bet she's beautiful."

Alex shrugged. "Yeah. Sure."

"You really don't like talking about your private life," Brianne said. "Either that or the relationship ended fairly recently . . ."

Or maybe I don't want to talk about my relationship with her when I still haven't been able to quell my attraction for you.

"I'm sorry I'm prying," Brianne said. "I'm just . . . making conversation."

Or was she curious? "Catarina and I were never meant to be. The relationship was nice, but I knew it would run its course."

"Not perfect enough for Mr. Perfect?"

She was smiling at him, and Alex didn't think the comment was serious. Still he said, "I'm not perfect. Hardly. I don't know. Maybe it could have worked, but she lives in Italy."

"Italy!"

"Yeah."

"You met her there?"

"Mmm hmm. After Carter . . . after he disappeared, I had to get away. I went to ski in Milan, and that's where I met her. She was a model."

"Ha! A model. So Carter was telling the truth." Brianne tried to keep her voice light, but Alex's revelation stung. She wasn't sure why.

"You travel a lot, stay at a lot of hotels, and you meet other people who travel a lot." Alex shrugged. "I've met a few models."

"I'm sure you were smitten with her," Brianne said. She forced a smile.

"We met on the slopes," Alex said. "She had just retired from modeling and decided to settle in Italy, so she could spend some time with her father's side of the family. She's biracial — part Italian, part Kenyan."

Brianne suddenly wanted Alex to stop talking. She didn't want to hear about his perfect relationship with this perfectly stunning woman.

"She sounds like the kind of woman men would go crazy for. Why didn't it work out? Only distance issues?"

"Among other things."

Brianne forced a laugh, though inside she felt anything but cheerful. She stared off at a pleasure boat in the distance. "Well, if a gorgeous model can't satisfy you, I'm not sure any woman can."

"What about you?" Alex asked.

Brianne's heart slammed against her chest. She didn't dare look at Alex. "Pardon me?"

"You haven't dated since Carter disappeared?"

Oh. That's what he meant. "No," she said, surprised to find that her voice came out as a croak. Her eyes followed the movements of the boat sailing in the Atlantic. "You know I haven't."

"Because you were still in love with him?"

Now that she was the one in the hot seat, she felt the way Alex apparently had — hesitant to talk.

"Are you?" Alex asked, his voice suddenly lower. "Are you still in love with Carter?"

Feeling the heat of his probing gaze, she turned, met his curious eyes. All she had to do was say yes. It would be so easy. And yet, that wouldn't quite be the truth.

The realization shocked her.

"It was hard, Alex," she said after several seconds. "Excruciatingly hard. I'd had so many hopes and dreams. How could I let it all go and think of dating? I wasn't like you. I didn't believe Carter was dead. Everyone may have said so, but in my heart, I never believed it."

"So you never stopped loving him." Alex was the one to look away now.

Brianne had the odd feeling that they were talking about something else. That they were saying one thing but meaning another.

"It was more like I didn't want to be hurt again. But yes, my heart was still his."

Abruptly, Alex turned from the railing and walked back into the bedroom. Brianne followed him, feeling as though she'd just said something wrong.

"Alex —"

"We should unpack," he said, not facing her as he continued to walk to the door. "Then, if you want, we can go out and get something to eat."

"Sure," Brianne said.

"It's too late to start our investigation tonight," Alex went on, "but tomorrow morning, bright and early, we can hit the ground running."

"Sounds good," Brianne said. But she was wondering why Alex didn't want to look at her.

Finally he did, holding her gaze for a long moment.

And then he walked out the door, leaving Brianne feeling out of sorts and wondering why.

CHAPTER 8

Brianne and Alex ended up heading out for dinner at a lively restaurant that had loud music and tasty food. It was the kind of place that didn't allow for intimate conversation.

Which was good. Because things had been weird once Alex had left Brianne in the bedroom.

She'd had the feeling he was upset at her for some reason, and continued to think so during dinner when they kept the conversation topics totally neutral. But as she'd lain awake in the large bed later that night, she began to see things differently.

Yes, Alex had cooled off. But it was the situation. The frustrating conundrum of finding a man they both loved and not knowing if it would happen.

Hadn't she herself experienced a roller coaster of emotions? One minute up, the next one down?

That's what she'd told herself all night long, but something about the inner dialogue didn't quite ring true.

And yet, what else could it be?

Around seven, Brianne woke up. She lay still in the bed, listening for any sounds that would tell her Alex was awake. After about five minutes of not a peep other than the cry of seagulls outside, she figured Alex was still asleep.

She got out of bed, stretched and walked to the terrace doors. As she swung them open to embrace the gorgeous view, she couldn't help thinking that she could seriously get used to waking up to this kind of view every day.

Stepping onto the terrace, she surveyed the vast ocean before her. That's when she noticed the person in the distance, jogging.

The person got closer, and Brianne felt a zap of awareness. Was that . . . ?

It was. She'd thought Alex was sleeping, but he was already up and getting in an early morning workout.

In shorts and sneakers.

He was naked from the waist up, his magnificent form gleaming with sweat.

As he got closer, he looked up as though he sensed her. Seeing her on the balcony, he waved. Brianne waved back, then she quickly retreated. She was only wearing a large T-shirt.

And Alex wasn't wearing one at all.

Lord have mercy.

Brianne continued to watch him through the window, feeling a little like a voyeur. But hey, he was the one out there with his shirt off.

And since when was it illegal to look at a gorgeous man?

When he neared his property, Brianne thought he would turn and head toward the house, but instead he kept jogging. She watched his back until he again became a dot in the distance.

Stepping away from the window, she contemplated a run on the beach herself. But what she really wanted to do right now was something to show her appreciation for Alex having brought her here. For his taking the initiative to find Carter.

So she went downstairs to the kitchen to see if there was anything in the fridge.

Honestly, she doubted she would find anything since they'd just arrived. Perhaps some hash browns in the freezer, and if she was lucky some eggs. But when she opened the large stainless steel fridge — complete with a flat-screen television built in the door — she saw that it was fully stocked with fresh produce and juice.

Clearly, someone had come by to stock the fridge with food before they arrived.

Brianne found a skillet, put it on the stove and placed some strips of turkey bacon in it to cook. Next, she got the coffee started. Then she set about cutting fresh apple slices and sectioning oranges and arranging them on a platter.

She was mixing eggs in a bowl to scramble them when she heard the patio door slide open. Whirling around, she saw Alex entering the house.

Heat zapped her body with the force of a Mack truck.

Lord have mercy . . .

Though she'd seen Alex from the terrace, seeing him up close — half naked — was something she wasn't prepared for. He was all hard muscles and ripples, and every inch of his upper body was gleaming with sweat. Forget a six-pack. Alex easily had an eight to ten-pack.

Good Lord, the man was sinfully sexy. All six-foot-four, decadent-chocolate inches of him.

He smiled as he regarded her, and Brianne's heart slammed against her rib cage. What was wrong with her?

"Morning, Bree."

Brianne tried to speak, but her throat was too dry for any sound to escape. Again, she couldn't help wondering what was wrong with her.

She reached for her mug of coffee and downed a liberal sip, wetting her throat.

"Hey," she managed. "That was one long run."

"Yeah." Alex blotted his face with a hand towel that he held. "I love starting my day with a run when I'm down here. Do you mind getting me a bottle of water from the fridge? I don't want to drip sweat all over the floor."

"Oh, sure." Brianne put the bowl of eggs down and scurried to the fridge, then brought a bottle of ice-cold water to Alex.

"Something smells good," Alex said as she handed it to him.

"I wanted to surprise you with breakfast."

"I can't wait to dig in. I'll get showered and be back in a bit."

When Alex turned and walked back outside, Brianne quickly asked, "Where are you going?"

"I've got a shower out here. Makes it easy."

Brianne's mind immediately conjured the image of an open-air shower, where Alex would stand naked as the day he was born, protected from prying eyes by only a few hedges or a short stone wall. And the image made her skin flush.

She couldn't help creeping to the patio doors and peering outside once she put the eggs in the skillet, but Alex was nowhere to be seen.

What am I doing?

Brianne went back to the stove before the eggs burned, mentally chiding herself for being so desperate for a glimpse of a naked Alex.

Clearly, it had been *way* too long since she'd had any action.

That would be rectified soon enough. Once she and Alex found Carter.

Provided Carter wasn't already involved with someone else.

The thought sobered Brianne as she finished scrambling the eggs. She was sharing portions on two plates when Alex appeared at the patio doors. He was wearing a T-shirt and long nylon track pants.

"Do you have a guest house out back?" she couldn't help asking as he entered the house, a hint of humor in her voice. Then again, she wouldn't be surprised if he did.

"A change room, sauna and a shower. It's much easier to jump in the shower out there when you've been in the pool or at the beach."

This kind of life was so foreign to Brianne, she could barely wrap her mind around it. And yet here she was, in Alex's magnificent *vacation* home.

"You really do lead a charmed life," she found herself saying.

"Don't confuse the things I have with the kind of life I live," Alex said. "I'm definitely blessed, I know that. But I work hard, travel a lot and don't always get to enjoy what I have. And there are times when all the money in the world can't buy you the happiness you want. Nor prevent bad things from happening."

"Like what happened to Carter," Brianne said softly.

Alex nodded. "And not just Carter."

There was a seriousness to his demeanor, one that told Brianne he was referring to something very painful that had happened in his life. But she didn't want to pry. She took the plates from the counter to the table, then went back for the coffee mugs. She was surprised when she turned and found Alex standing directly in her path.

"My mother died when I was eighteen," Alex said. No preamble, no warning and no particular emotion. But as Brianne looked into his eyes, she could see the pain there. And she wanted to wrap her arms around him and hug him, the only comfort she could offer.

"I'm sorry," she said.

"I don't know why I'm telling you this. I don't really talk about her passing. But you . . . I like talking to you. You're a good listener."

Brianne was surprised — and touched. She figured for sure that Alex thought her nosey after she asked him about girlfriends last night. It meant a lot that he actually trusted her enough to share this with him.

"How?" Her tone was gentle. "What happened?"

"Lupus," he replied, agony twisting his face. "We always knew the day would come, but . . ."

"But you're never prepared for it," Brianne finished for him.

Alex shook his head, not speaking.

"You were close," Brianne said, knowing with certainty that they were.

"Very."

"I can't imagine . . . I can't imagine losing a parent." She wanted to hug him, and yet she didn't want to behave inappropriately. The last thing she wanted to do was lead him on.

"What I regret most is that she died before I made something of myself. She always believed in me. I wish she'd been able to live longer, that I could have spoiled her with nice things."

"I'm sure your love was enough," Brianne said. "She knew you loved her, and that's what would have meant the most to her."

Alex's jaw flinched, and for a moment Brianne wondered if he were angry. But why would he be angry at a time like this, after speaking so fondly about his mother?

"The breakfast's getting cold," she announced, changing the subject before the mood became too grim. "If you grab the coffee carafe, we'll be set."

"Sure," Alex said, but he sounded distracted.

Moments later they were both sitting at the round glass table in the kitchen, eating in silence. Brianne was glad when Alex lifted a remote control from the center of the table and turned on the refrigerator's TV — even if she wasn't particularly interested in the fluff piece on CNN.

Several minutes later, Brianne spoke after washing down some turkey bacon with coffee. "Thank you." At Alex's confused expression, she quickly explained. "For coming to me with the news about Carter possibly being alive. I know I wasn't sure if I wanted to be involved in this when you told me about it, but I have no doubts now. This is exactly where I need to be. Where I want to be. So thank you."

Alex nodded as he chewed a mouthful of food.

"What's the plan for today?" Brianne went on.

Alex swallowed and then said, "I have the address for Dean Knight's office. It opens at ten. I say we get there right when it opens."

Brianne glanced at the digital clock on the stove. It was 8:34. "So in ninety minutes, we'll get some answers." She drew in an unsteady breath. "By the end of the day, we could be reunited with Carter."

CHAPTER 9

No question, Florida was one of the most beautiful states. Maybe it was that stunning view of the water — both from Alex's house and as they drove along North Atlantic Avenue — but Brianne had never seen a prettier view.

Alex turned right along West International Speedway, and they traveled over a bridge that took them to part of Daytona that was separated from the beach. This city was sprawling, from what Brianne could tell. Businesses were not crowded together, but rather spaced apart. Maybe that was because the city planners had left enough space for beautiful flowers and greenery to line the streets.

Alex made a series of turns off of the main thoroughfare and ultimately ended up on a street named Orange. At five minutes after ten — precisely twenty minutes after they had pulled out of Alex's driveway — Alex pulled up in front of a moderate-size two-story house. Also different from the city of Buffalo, Brianne noted that many of the businesses in Daytona were converted houses. Or perhaps they had been designed to look like houses from the beginning. Whatever the case, she liked the look. The colors were bright and warm and welcoming.

"This is it?" Brianne asked. Though it was obvious. A sign on the building read DEAN KNIGHT ENTERPRISE.

"Yep." Alex turned off the car's ignition and faced her. "Don't be nervous."

It was then that Brianne realized she was tightly clenching her fingers together. She loosened them. "It's just suddenly so real."

"Answers. That's why we're here."

"You have the pictures?" Alex had shown her a handful of photos that he had printed of Carter.

"Yeah. I've got them." He removed the small envelope from the glove compartment. "Are you ready?"

Brianne nodded.

Alex exited the car door and came around to the passenger side. He opened the door for Brianne, who had been sitting there. Not waiting for him to be chivalrous, but sitting, frozen, in a state of sheer panic.

What if Alex were wrong? What if they had come this way only to learn the Carter he had seen was some other person altogether?

"It's okay, Brianne," Alex said gently. "No matter what happens."

She nodded shakily. "What if Dean's not here?"

"See that Ferrari in the driveway? It's the same one I saw on television. He's here."

She was stalling, she knew.

Alex offered her his hand. "Come on."

Brianne accepted Alex's hand, noting just how strong it was. He helped her down from the Navigator, but didn't release her hand once her feet were securely on the ground. And she didn't pull her hand away. She held Alex's hand, taking strength from him as they both went up the walkway to the front door.

There was an exterior screen door, through which they could see into the office, given that the interior door was open. Alex had explained that Dean Knight had created a charitable foundation to help children with autism, an issue near and dear to his heart since he had a younger brother who was autistic.

There was a glamorous black woman sitting behind a high glass counter. She looked at Brianne first — then her eyes widened with interest when they landed on Alex. Her subsequent smile was warm, and perhaps a bit flirtatious.

"May I help you?" she asked. She fluffed her long hair, looking only at Alex.

Oh, yeah. She was flirting.

Alex rested his elbows on the counter, leaning forward. "Yeah, you can." He returned her smile, and it was all dazzle. "I'm here to see Dean Knight."

The receptionist looked down at a large desk calendar. "Do you have an appointment?"

"No, I'm sorry. I didn't get to make one." His voice was deep and sultry. "Will that be a problem . . . or can you help me out?"

Brianne narrowed her eyes as she stared at Alex. Oh, my God. *He* was flirting right back.

"I'll see what I can do. You're lucky he's in today. Tomorrow he heads to California."

"Lucky me."

Why are you standing there making goo-goo eyes with this woman? Brianne wanted to ask. *Can we get on with this already?*

"What's your name?" the woman asked.

"Alex. Alex Thorpe. And your name is?"

"Ginny."

"Nice to meet you, Ginny."

Brianne crossed her arms over her chest

and barely stopped herself from rolling her eyes. It was as if she wasn't even there.

Ginny stood, revealing a perfect hourglass figure tightly clad in a black minidress. Brianne couldn't help it — she felt a spate of jealousy.

"Can I tell Mr. Knight what this is in regards to?"

"It's a personal matter."

Ginny blushed, as if Alex had just told her that he wanted to whisper sweet nothings in her ear.

Seriously?

"Give me a minute," Ginny said. "I'll see if Mr. Knight can spare some time."

Ginny strutted off, revealing superlong legs accented by sexy black heels. Brianne was certain she was exaggerating her hip sway for Alex's benefit.

Alex turned to Brianne and said, "That went well."

"Hmm."

"What?" Alex asked.

"Nothing."

"Why do you seem upset?"

Brianne blew out a harried breath. What was wrong with her? Why *did* she feel upset?

"Because we're here to find Carter and you're . . . *flirting*." She felt ridiculous for saying the words, and yet she couldn't stop herself.

"Sometimes a little flirtation goes a long way."

As if to emphasize that point, Ginny returned, her ear-to-ear smile revealing that she had good news. "Mr. Knight will see you," she announced.

"Great," Alex said. "Thank you, Ginny."

"Follow me, please."

Brianne wouldn't be surprised to learn that Ginny had forgotten she was even there, it was so clear that the woman had eyes only for Alex.

So what? Brianne asked herself. It wasn't like it mattered. If Alex had made a love connection, good for him.

Dean Knight was standing when Alex and Brianne entered his office behind Ginny. He was noticeably shorter than Alex. Though most men who stood next to Alex were.

He looked part Caucasian, part Asian and one hundred percent cute. Brianne could only imagine that women threw themselves at him. Women who loved men who lived on the edge.

It was the one thing she *hadn't* liked about Carter, though she'd fallen for everything else. She never liked his living on the edge,

134

always fearing it would be the death of him.

"My assistant says you want to see me," Dean said, his eyes registering caution.

Alex walked toward him, his hand outstretched. "Hey, man. How you doing?"

Dean shook Alex's hand, still looking guarded. "I'm good. Do I know you?"

"I'm Alex Thorpe," Alex said. "And this is my friend, Brianne Kenyon."

"Hi." Brianne raised her hand in a small wave.

Dean acknowledged her with a nod, then gestured to the two chairs on one side of a large mahogany desk. "Please, have a seat."

Brianne and Alex did as he suggested, settling into the plush leather seats. Dean walked around to the other side of his desk and took a seat opposite them. "Now, how can I help you?"

"A few weeks ago, I called you," Alex explained. "At the time I asked you if you knew a Carter Smith."

Dean's eyes registered understanding. "Right. I remember." He paused. "I also remember telling you that I didn't know anyone by that name."

"I know you did, but I'm thinking you might know him by another name. I brought some pictures with me. All I want you to do is look at them and see if the guy in the pictures is someone you know."

"Look, I don't want to get in the middle of anything," Dean said. His expression was still guarded.

"The guy we're looking for is a friend. We . . . lost touch. I'm just trying to reach out to him. If it *is* him."

Alex spoke casually, and Brianne could see the tension in Dean's shoulders ebbing away. "Let me see the pics."

Alex withdrew the handful of photos from the envelope and passed them across the desk to Dean. Dean flipped through them, giving a good five seconds of attention to each of the first few before skimming the others.

Shaking his head, he passed the photos back to Alex. "Naw. He doesn't look familiar."

"Are you sure?" Alex asked.

"I don't know him," Dean said, his tone leaving no room for doubt. "I'm sorry you wasted your time coming here."

"Wait." Brianne quickly reached into her purse and pulled out her wallet. Opening it, she withdrew a photo. Alex could see that it was a picture of her and Carter. He didn't know why, but it bugged him to know that she was carrying around such a photo.

Of course he knew why. Because Carter

was not worthy of her undying admiration.

"This is another picture of Carter," Brianne explained. "As you can see, he's got a goatee in this photo — which he didn't have in the photos that Alex showed you. Try to look at the facial structure. He might have gained or lost weight —"

"I said I don't know who he is."

Dean spoke abruptly, almost as if he were annoyed. Alex knew that the man was busy, but something about his tone and body language set off an alarm in Alex's brain.

He was lying. Alex didn't know why, but he was certain of that fact.

"Well, you know someone who looks like him," Brianne insisted. "Alex saw him. He saw him on television with you. You've got to know —"

Dean raised his palms in a helpless gesture. "I don't know what you want me to say. If I don't know the guy, I don't know the guy."

"But —"

Alex put a hand on Brianne's arm. "Brianne, he doesn't know him."

Brianne looked at Alex, her eyes large and glistening with tears. "But you said —"

"I know what I said. But I was obviously mistaken." Alex looked at Dean as he said the last word.

Dean nodded. "Exactly. I see a lot of people, man. Sometimes they run down to see me after a race. I don't know who they all are. This guy — even if he was on the track that day — I don't know him."

Brianne wanted to cry. And she wanted to scream. Alex was giving up so easily. Why walk away now? After they had come so far?

Besides, she got the impression that Dean was hiding something. She wasn't sure why — it was just a sense she had. Now was the time to stress to Dean just how important it was that they find Carter. Not simply act like they were two old friends in town hoping to touch base with him.

Alex stood. Reaching across the desk, he shook Dean's hand. "Thanks for your time."

Brianne stared at Alex in a state of disbelief.

"Come on, Brianne. We've taken up enough of Mr. Knight's time."

She didn't move. Instead she tried to convey with her eyes her desire that they stay and press Dean harder. But when Alex extended his hand to her, she reluctantly stood.

"Sorry I couldn't be of help," Dean said.

"Hey, if you don't know him, you don't know him."

Alex placed a hand on Brianne's elbow

and guided her toward the door, as if he didn't trust her to go of her own free will.

"Take care," Dean called out as they reached the door to his office.

Alex responded, but Brianne didn't bother to even turn and acknowledge him as Alex ushered her out of the office. She was suddenly angry. With Dean Knight and with Alex.

"Going so soon?" Ginny asked.

"Yeah," Alex told her. "Thanks for your help."

"Anytime." Ginny fluttered her unnaturally long eyelashes.

Brianne wanted to throw something.

"Brianne, will you wait for me outside?" Alex asked.

Her eyes grew wide in astonishment. But when she saw the megawatt smile on Ginny's face, she knew the deal.

"Fine," she said tersely.

Brianne turned and marched out the door. She thought she heard Ginny say a goodbye, but she wasn't sure.

Brianne stomped all the way to the car, yanked on the door, but found it locked. Silently she cursed.

"If you leave me out here waiting forever . . ."

Two minutes that seemed like two hours

passed. Then the front door opened. Alex casually made his way down the steps, looking as if he didn't have a care in the world.

"I see you have your priorities straight," Brianne muttered as Alex reached her.

"Excuse me?"

"We're here to find Carter, but you seem more interested in making a love connection with Ginny."

"Brianne —"

"And Dean says he doesn't recognize Carter, and you just say, okay fine, let's go? Why exactly did you have me come down here with you if you were going to give up so easily? What was the point?"

"Brianne —"

"After getting my hopes up, telling me you were certain, you now you think you were mistaken. So does that mean you think you were wrong about Carter being alive?"

Alex pressed a finger to Brianne's lips to silence her. "Bree, stop talking for a second and hear me out."

"No," Brianne said, stepping away from Alex's touch. It looked to him like she was going to cry. "This is exactly what I was worried about. Coming down here on a wild goose chase. I got my hopes up, and now —"

"He's lying," Alex said, and that stopped

her cold. "Dean Knight lied about not recognizing Carter."

Brianne's eyes widened, her lips parting in surprise. "So it's not just me?" she asked. "You felt it, too."

"He tried to hide it, but I saw the recognition in his eyes when he looked at the picture of Carter. He knows him."

"Then what are we doing out here?" Brianne asked. "We need to go back inside, get him to fess up."

Brianne took a step in the direction of Dean's office, but Alex reached out and grabbed her arm, stopping her. "No. We're not going back in there. Not yet."

Confusion streaked across Brianne's face. "I don't understand."

"Brianne, we came down here to find out if Carter is alive." Alex couldn't help grinning. "Let's not lose sight of the big picture. The fact that Dean's lying is good news. Because it means what I thought was true. Carter's alive."

CHAPTER 10

Alex was smiling like the cat who ate the canary. "He's alive, Brianne. He's alive."

Slowly, realization dawned on Brianne. She got it. "Oh, my God, you're right. I never thought of it that way. He would only lie if he knows who Carter is."

"Exactly."

Brianne frowned. "But I don't understand. If Carter was lost on a mountain three years ago, why would Dean lie about knowing him?"

"He shouldn't. But maybe Dean's the kind of guy who doesn't like answering questions asked by random strangers. He doesn't know us. That could be affecting his decision to say anything. Remember, his first words were that he didn't want to get in the middle of anything. He might assume we're looking for Carter for some untoward reason."

"If you're right," Brianne began, "then

how do we get through to this guy?"

"We could follow him." Alex paused, thought for a bit. "See if he goes straight to Carter. Of course, he might just call him. Or maybe I'm wrong and he doesn't know who Carter is."

"Do you believe that?"

"No. I think he knows something. If I had to guess, I would assume that he figures Carter is in some kind of trouble. Maybe a guy who's wanted by the cops for some reason, and that's where his hesitation is coming from." Alex shrugged. "I think that makes the most sense."

"So, what should we do?"

Alex pursed his lips. "I asked Ginny if she recognized the photos of Carter, and she said no. I believed her but left her my information in case she learns something that can help us."

"I'm sure you'll be hearing from her regardless," Brianne muttered.

"Pardon me?"

"Nothing," she said. Seriously, why was she feeling uncomfortable at the idea of Alex and Ginny getting together?

"You know, maybe you're right," Alex said after a moment. "Maybe we should go back in there."

"Right now?" But before Brianne even got

the question out, Alex took her hand in his and started back up the stairs to the office. Moments later, Alex was striding past the receptionist, smiling sweetly at her and apologizing profusely. He walked right into Dean's office.

The look on Dean's face was more than surprised. It was as though he had been caught with his hand in the cookie jar. "When you get this message," Dean said quickly into the phone, "call me back."

"Was that Carter you called?" Alex asked.

Dean didn't answer right away. "I already told you —"

Alex advanced. "You and I both know that you're lying about recognizing him. I'm not saying I blame you. You're obviously a good friend, having his back like that. But in case you think we're here because we've got a beef with Carter, or because he's wanted for something illegal, rest assured that is not the case. We simply are trying to track him down. We're friends of his from . . . from way back. Mostly, we want to know that he is okay."

"Please," Brianne said, "if you know something, you've got to tell us. I was his fiancée."

Dean's eyes widen slightly, as though Brianne's words had surprised him. Still, he didn't speak, just stared.

Alex passed Dean a card. "This is my name and all my info. Enough to go to the cops with if you think I'm out to harm Carter."

Dean accepted the card, staring at it for a moment, then meeting Alex's eyes once again. He exhaled sharply and said, "The guy I know, his name isn't Carter."

"So you do know him," Alex said. Obviously his decision to give Dean his contact information had assured him that he was trustworthy.

"I don't know him well," Dean answered. "But if it's the same guy, I know him as Donnie. Loves the racing circuit. He's a friend of a friend. That's who I was calling when you walked in the door."

"Who's this friend?" Alex asked.

"Someone who's out of the country right now."

"And he can tell us where to find Carter?"

Dean stared at Alex, then at Brianne. He was sizing them up, as if still trying to decide if he could totally trust what they told him. "How do I know this business card is real?"

"It's real. Call my phone right now if you want. I'm the owner of several sporting goods stores across the country and in some international locations. I've never had a speeding ticket, much less been arrested. No — that's not true. I did get one speeding ticket when I was twenty."

Dean's expression relaxed somewhat. "Where I come from, you don't just go telling people things when you don't know who they are. This guy is a friend of a friend, and I don't want to see him get hurt."

"Like I said," Alex began, "we don't want to hurt him. We're friends who lost touch some years back."

Dean's eyes fell on Brianne. "You said you used to be his fiancée."

"I did. I was his fiancée."

"And here you are, trying to find him." Dean said the words almost like an accusation.

"I'm perfectly aware that he's likely moved on, but we didn't end things on a . . . sour note. In fact —"

Alex gently nudged Brianne, silently urging her not to divulge too much information. "Why don't we do this? If you get in touch with your friend, you can tell him that I came by looking for Carter — Donnie — and leave it up to him to call me."

Nodding, Dean once again glanced at the card Alex had handed him. "All right. I can do that, man."

"Thanks." Alex offered Dean his hand, and the two exchanged a hearty handshake. Alex could tell he'd gotten through to Dean.

When they were outside, Brianne said, "You think he'll pass along your info?"

"I think so. Talking to him a second time, I get the sense that he believes us. He's just trying to look out for his friend's friend." He paused. *"Donnie."*

Brianne rounded the car. "If Carter's using the name Donnie, then he definitely doesn't know who he is."

"Hmm," Alex responded noncommittally. He pressed the car's remote to unlock the car. He could think of another reason to explain why he was using a different name.

Brianne spoke again when she was sitting in the passenger seat. "Was it just me, or did Dean look shocked when I said I was Carter's fiancée?" She didn't wait for Alex to answer. "I know I should be prepared for the fact that Carter has a whole new life — I keep telling myself that — but it's hard to believe he could have a girlfriend or a wife and have completely forgotten me."

"You know that's a possibility," Alex said. "Yes, we're here looking for Carter, but I think it's important for both of us to accept that he's not going to be who he was three

147

years ago."

"I know, but . . ." Brianne's voice trailed off.

"But what?"

"I'm scared."

Damn if she didn't sound all soft and vulnerable. Again, Alex wondered if it had been wrong to involve her in this at all. He knew that if they found Carter, Brianne would be devastated.

Provided her feelings for him were the same as they had been three years ago.

"I know you're scared," he said. "But I'm here for you. I want you to know that. Whatever happens, I'm here for you."

Alex didn't think. Just reached for her hand and gave it a comforting squeeze.

Warmth shot through his body. Touching Brianne was like touching a live wire. Of course it was. He was attracted to her — that much he had accepted years ago. What he didn't understand was why the attraction hadn't faded over time. After all, it wasn't like he'd had a chance with her.

"He'll want to come back to me, right?" Brianne asked, driving home the point that Alex's feelings for her were unrequited. "Maybe not right away, but eventually? Best-case scenario, he'll look at me and remember everything — our life together, everything we shared — and he'll want that back. Or am I being completely ridiculous?"

Alex pulled his hand away and faced forward. "It might happen."

"But you don't believe it."

"Bree, I'm not sure what to believe. Like I said, we both have to be prepared for anything when we find Carter."

Glancing at Brianne, he saw that her mouth was quivering. *Fragile.* That's the word that jumped into his brain.

Did she honestly believe that she and Carter would be able to pick up where they'd left off? What kind of fairytale world was she living in?

And yet, seeing her on the verge of falling apart, there was a part of him that wanted to tell her exactly what she wanted to hear. Another part of him felt guilty as hell for involving her in this. Perhaps he should tell her to return to Buffalo, that he would continue the search on his own. Because he was suddenly realizing just how much the truth would hurt her, and he didn't want to break her heart.

Of course, he couldn't be positive of the outcome. But in his heart he knew they would learn that Carter wasn't an unfortunate victim of nature but a coldhearted liar.

"I really do appreciate you being here for

me," Brianne said as Alex started the Navigator. "You're . . ." Her voice cracked slightly. "You're a great friend."

Alex looked away, Brianne's words making him feel like the biggest jerk on the planet. Damn. This was bad. Brianne was far too emotionally vulnerable to deal with this.

Before Alex had gone to see her about the possibility of Carter being alive, he had considered the consequences of involving her. He'd figured that yes, she would be upset if things played out the way he suspected, but now he knew it would be worse than that.

This search for Carter had the potential to be more than simply upsetting. It could hurt Brianne beyond measure. The kind of hurt she might not get over with a good cry.

She had held out hope beyond reason that she would be reunited with Carter, even when it was completely unlikely that that would ever happen. She hadn't wanted to give up hope, not even for a second. And she hadn't dated since, a clear indicator that her love for Carter hadn't died.

Given her level of devotion to her former fiancé, learning the truth about him could send Brianne into an emotional tailspin. Why hadn't Alex seen that?

He had always planned to be there for her to help her through the aftermath of finding Carter. He just didn't consider that the aftermath could be total emotional hell for Brianne.

"Hey," Brianne said softly.

Alex faced her. "Yeah?"

She offered him a tentative smile. "I appreciate you being here for me. I'm not sure I could get through this if not for you."

Damn, Alex silently cursed. He was seeing, pretty much for the first time, that this plan of his could backfire. As much as he had planned to be there for Brianne, he now realized that she might not forgive him.

"You want to head back to my place and wait for Dean's friend to call?" Alex asked. "Or if you want, I can take you sightseeing. That might be a good way to pass the time."

"I'm not in the mood for sightseeing. I think I'd like to go to the house and lie down."

"You okay?"

"Yeah. I'm fine." But she didn't look at him as she said the words. "I just need . . . a mental break."

Lord, she was vulnerable and sweet. She deserved someone who would love and adore her and never betray her. Alex wanted to draw her into his arms, tell her to forget

Carter, to show her with his embrace that *he* was the one who would love and protect her forever.

And yet, instead of protecting her, he was going to have to break her heart. By this time tomorrow — if they found Carter — instead of looking at him with appreciation, Brianne might just look at him with hate.

CHAPTER 11

Brianne spent the next few hours in the bedroom, lying under the covers but not sleeping.

Her brain was on overdrive, a myriad of thoughts keeping her unsettled.

She was scared suddenly. Truly scared about what the future held. And not just because Carter could easily have a girlfriend or a wife.

She was scared of what *she* would feel when she saw him again.

Or rather, what she might not feel.

She cared for Carter and always would, but the more she tried to imagine a life with him again, the harder it was. If she was entirely honest with herself, her feelings for him weren't the same as they'd been three years ago. They weren't the same as they'd been a year ago.

When Alex had come to see her, she had been on the verge of moving forward with her life. Carter was still in her heart, but she had come to accept that she couldn't spend the rest of her life pining over him. It was time that she open her heart to love again.

She was here in Daytona hoping to find Carter, but she was starting to think that she was here more out of a sense of obligation as opposed to a heartfelt desire to reconnect with the love of her life.

Maybe she was just having jitters — similar to the kind a bride had before she walked down the aisle. Maybe it was simply the unknown she was afraid of.

Brianne rolled onto her other side, facing the window. The sky was blue and the sun was bright. And here she was in the bedroom, lying in bed as if she were sick.

She climbed out of bed. She would go outside and enjoy the day. Take a swim in the gorgeous pool in Alex's stunning backyard.

Maybe he would join her.

Brianne's stomach fluttered at the thought of seeing him again, as if two weeks had passed instead of two hours.

She went to her suitcase and found her bathing suit. As she slipped into it and stared at her reflection, she couldn't help wondering what Alex would think when he saw her.

Would he find her sexy the way he obviously thought Ginny was?

What do you care what he thinks about how you look?

But even though that was Brianne's rational thought, as she dressed in the bright red bikini, she secretly hoped that Alex liked it.

Alex had his iPhone to his ear when he heard the soft footfalls on the marble floor. He eased forward on the recliner where he sat in the living room, angling his head to the left.

And then a searing jolt of heat flooded his groin.

Brianne was walking toward him wearing a two-piece bathing suit in fire engine red. The suit couldn't have screamed "Look at my hot body" more loudly.

And it was hot. The curves were still there. Slimmer than when he'd known her years ago, but they were evident nonetheless.

"Wyatt, I'll call you back," he said into the phone, then disconnected the call before his business associate could even reply.

As Brianne moved closer to him, Alex's eyes traveled over that lush body of hers, which was partially covered by a beach robe. The robe was open at the front, giving Alex all the view he wanted. Brianne's breasts were full beneath the bikini top, showing a tantalizing amount of skin at her cleavage. Her waist was narrow, but her hips were also full. She had the perfect hourglass figure.

Honest to God, Carter was a fool. He had taken Brianne for granted, and it didn't make a lick of sense to Alex. Not just because she was gorgeous, but because she was loyal and sweet.

Brianne fiddled with her robe, pulling it closed. A reaction to the way he had blatantly ogled her? But surely she had known that he would check out her fine body. She wouldn't have come downstairs in a bikini like that and not expected him to check her out.

"You don't mind if I use your pool, do you?" she asked.

"No." The word came out as a croak, and Alex cleared his throat. "Naw. Of course not."

Brianne started toward the patio doors, and it was then that Alex saw the gold sandals on her feet. He had never considered himself a foot guy, but her feet were seriously cute. He loved those pale pink toenails.

"Wait," Alex said, and quickly got to his

feet. "Let me show you where the towels are."

Brianne stepped outside, where she waited for him to join her. She slipped off her robe and placed it on the back of a chair — and all of Alex's air left his lungs in a rush.

The bikini bottom was high cut, which he had seen from the front. He should have known that the cut of the piece would expose an ample amount of her behind.

And what a sweet behind it was . . .

Damn, you're beautiful.

Brianne whirled around and looked up at him. "You really think so?"

Aw, hell. He'd spoken his thought aloud.

"I'm sorry," she went on before he could speak. "You said I should just accept a compliment, so that's what I'm going to do." She grinned. "Thank you."

Alex was tempted to touch her. To reach out and stroke her arms. To curl his fingers around her neck and pull her toward him. To kiss those ridiculously sexy lips of hers until they both were gasping for air.

Get a grip, man. So what if she has a hot body? She's not into you, so forget it.

But regardless of his thought, he could feel the surefire evidence of his desire for her growing in his drawers — something he could not control. He quickly walked across the patio to the small house at the side of the backyard, thankful he was wearing loose-fitting athletic pants and hoping against hope that Brianne hadn't sensed or seen the direction of his thoughts.

The small house had a bathroom with a shower on one side and a sauna on the other. Alex opened the door and turned — and once again felt the full force of his attraction for Brianne when he saw her standing right behind him.

Didn't she know she was killing him? Standing so close to him like that and giving him a full view of her newly toned body? What would she do if he pulled her in his arms and kissed her? Would she pull away? Or would her lips melt against his?

"Ah, the towels are right there," Brianne said, looking beyond him into the bathroom. "Great."

"Like I said yesterday, you can shower off in here. You access the sauna through the other door. If you want to use it, you turn the knob here to heat it."

"Why don't you join me?" Brianne asked.

"Join you?" Nervous, Alex swallowed, his body responding as if she'd asked him to get naked with her.

"Yeah. We can do a few laps together."

Alex shrugged, trying his best to appear

nonchalant. "Okay. Yeah. Yeah, sure."

Brianne grinned widely. "Great."

She walked to the pool's edge, and Alex watched her dip one beautiful foot into the water. "Oooh, it's nice and warm."

"I don't like cold pools," Alex explained. Though right about now he would do well with a cold shower.

"Salt water?" she asked.

"Yep. Like the ocean."

"Nice." Brianne jumped right in, no hesitation, her entire body immersing in the water. She wasn't like most women he knew, who would get into the water to their shoulders, fearful of wetting their hair. When she burst through the water's surface, her short bob clung to her head, the strands already wavy.

"What are you waiting for?" Brianne asked.

Alex didn't need any further prompting.

He hurried upstairs to his bedroom, changed into black swimming trunks, then quickly made his way back to the pool.

Brianne greeted him with her warm smile, and Alex's breath caught in his throat. Every time he looked at her, he was more and more smitten.

He was attracted to her outer beauty, yes, but it was her inner beauty that had won him over.

Alex jumped into the water, creating a waterfall of splashes. Brianne giggled and wiped at her eyes. And then she scooped up handfuls of water and threw it at Alex.

"Hey," he protested good-naturedly.

"You splashed me first."

"Unintentionally."

"I'm not sure I believe that." But she was smiling, telling him that she was in a playful mood.

One minute he had been certain she would spend the rest of the day in the bedroom alone. The next she was shocking him by walking into the living room in her bathing suit.

"Wanna race?" Alex asked, her playful mood rubbing off on him.

Before she could respond, he dove forward, swimming for the farthest end of the pool. He could hear Brianne behind him, doing her best to keep pace.

He hit the far wall, stopped and was surprised to see that Brianne was only a couple of lengths behind him. She'd given him a run for his money.

"What are you, a dolphin?" he asked as she joined him at the wall.

"My family always said so. I can spend hours at a time in the water. When I was getting back into shape, one of the things I did was swim daily."

"Come on, Brianne. You were never out of shape."

"You didn't see me after Carter's one-year memorial. I hit a real low then, not believing him dead but feeling totally helpless in terms of finding him. I turned to food — the one thing that wouldn't let me down." She paused. "I gained over thirty pounds."

"Wow," Alex said, truly surprised. "I find that very hard to believe."

"Believe it. But once my sister got engaged, I knew I wanted to shape up once and for all. I started to eat better and worked out every day. I don't believe in counting calories and depriving myself. But I do know how to control the urge to overeat. At least I think I do."

"If you lost more than thirty pounds, then you're obviously doing something right."

Brianne swam leisurely on her back to the center of the pool, and Alex indulged in the view. With her breasts pointing to the sky, all he could think was how much he wanted to remove that skimpy bikini and feel her wet, naked body against his.

In the center of the pool, she swung her body upright and began to tread water. Alex swam to her.

He was about to slip his arm around her waist — he seriously wanted to — but then she asked, "Is that the phone?"

"The phone? Oh, heck. The phone." Alex swam to the steps and hurriedly exited the pool. He walked quickly to the patio door, straining to hear the sound of his iPhone.

But he heard nothing. If the phone had been ringing, it had stopped.

No point going into the house soaking wet. He went to the outdoor shower, retrieved a towel and went inside to get his phone. A quick look at the screen told him he had indeed missed a call. But when he checked the number, he saw that Wyatt had called from Phoenix. It wasn't a call having to do with Carter.

He brought the phone outside with him and placed it on the table. Brianne was at the edge of the pool, waiting for him.

"Was that Dean?" she asked.

"No. It was a call for work," Alex explained.

Brianne heaved herself out of the pool and sat on the side. "Do you mind getting me a towel?" she asked.

"Not at all." Alex made his way to the bathroom, where he pulled out one of his big, fluffy towels. By the time he brought it to Brianne, she was standing. He opened the towel and wrapped it around her.

She smiled up at him softly, a twinkle in her eyes. "Thanks."

Something tugged at Alex's heart. And he wondered, not for the first time, if Brianne felt anything toward him other than friendship. There were times when she'd give him a certain look or a smile and he was certain that yes, she was attracted to him as well. She was wrapped up in the idea of reconnecting with Carter, but Alex couldn't help wondering if her heart was no longer with his former best friend.

Couldn't help hoping that.

"What do you expect when you see Carter again?" Brianne asked suddenly, as if she had sensed where his thoughts had gone.

A beat passed. Then Alex said, "I don't really know."

"It's different for you," Brianne said. She used the towel to dry her hair. "You were buddies. There's no reason you can't go back to being buddies." She hugged the towel around her body. "But for me . . ."

Her voice trailed off. She didn't finish her statement, just stared at a point beyond Alex's shoulder.

"What?" Alex prompted. "What were you going to say?"

"I'm so up and down over the whole situation," she said. "One minute I'm trying to convince myself that everything will go back to the way it was with Carter. The next I'm sure I'm fooling myself. I can't expect everything to be the way it was."

"One day at a time, remember?"

Brianne took a few steps past him, and Alex was sure he heard her mumble something that sounded like *I'm not sure I want it to be the way it was.*

Had he heard her correctly? Or was he hearing things? "What'd you say?"

Slowly Brianne turned and met Alex's gaze. "Nothing. I'm totally being silly."

Alex closed the distance between them, hope filling him. "Did you say that you're not sure you want it to be the way it was?"

"I told you I'm being silly. Letting paranoia get to me. Wondering what will happen if he doesn't recognize me, or worse, if he's got a girlfriend." She paused. Looked into Alex's eyes. And damn if he didn't see that spark again — a spark of attraction.

Brianne jerked her gaze away and walked to the pool's edge. "But I can't worry about any of that, right? I have to have faith that we're here for a reason, and that everything will work out fine."

Alex got the feeling she was saying what

she thought she should say. What she believed was expected of her. Not thinking about his actions, he walked to her and circled his arms around her from behind.

She tensed. "Alex . . ."

What had come over him? He began to loosen his arms, but Brianne suddenly turned, placing her hands on his chest. This time when she gazed up at him, there was no mistaking the look in her eyes. There was a definite spark of heat.

Either that or Alex was losing his mind.

The heat was burning his skin, and Alex wanted nothing more than to kiss her. And he was about to do just that — until Brianne suddenly looked away.

"Look at me," Alex said softly.

Brianne raised her eyes to his. And what she saw in his gaze surprised her.

Raw heat.

The heat ignited her own. Almost surprisingly, she leaned into him, *wanting* to feel his body pressed against her own. She didn't understand it. She only knew that she wanted it.

And when he lowered his lips to hers, Brianne held her breath. Oh, she wanted this. More than she had wanted anything in a long, long time.

His lips grazed hers. A light touch, but

one that made her feel she'd been jolted by a zap of electricity. And in that instant, she was alive suddenly. Alive with sensations she hadn't felt in three years.

Alex hesitated only for a second before claiming her mouth with force. Hungrily, as if he'd waited to do this for a lifetime.

His tongue delved into her mouth, wet and hot, and Brianne braced her hands on his naked chest. She felt the strong muscles there, and a little thrill shot through her. How long had it been since she had kissed a man?

Too long.

He tightened his arms around her waist and pulled her against him, while his tongue twisted with hers.

She was lost in the sensations. Lost in the passion. But when one of Alex's hands moved from her back to the side of her breast, Brianne had a sudden wake-up call.

What am I doing?

She was here to find Carter, not to get it on with Alex.

She pulled back, stepping out of his arms. Alex's eyes were heavy-lidded, the desire evident in their dark depths. He hadn't wanted to stop.

Brianne turned away from him, unable to handle the reality she saw in his eyes.

Because she had felt the same way. She hadn't wanted to stop.

Which only made her wonder what had gotten into her.

"Um," she began, not sure what to truly say. "I . . . I don't know how that happened, but let's just forget that it did."

Alex didn't say anything, and Brianne turned. She gasped when she saw that he was standing right behind her.

"What if I don't want to forget?" Alex asked.

"You don't mean that," Brianne said, her voice barely a whisper, hardly holding any conviction at all. "How close are we to finding Carter? Very. So . . . what happened between us doesn't make sense."

Alex took a step toward her, and Brianne instinctively took a step back. "What if I said that it makes perfect sense?"

Brianne's heart slammed against her rib cage. What was Alex doing? Testing her? Or had he fallen off the bed in the night and hit his head?

"You mean because . . ." Again, he stepped toward her, and she took another step backward. "Because . . . because we're spending so much time together."

Another step. Then another. Brianne's legs

bumped into a patio chair, forcing her to stop.

"Something like that," Alex said. His voice was low and husky, and good Lord, it was turning her on.

"Alex . . . we need to . . ." Brianne's words trailed off on a breathless sigh when Alex actually stepped backward.

Though Brianne had told herself that this was exactly what she wanted — some breathing space — she suddenly missed his presence.

"Maybe you're right," he said.

Brianne looked up at him, disappointed. Wasn't she the one who had broken the kiss? So why on earth was she disappointed?

Her heart began to pound. Good Lord, she wanted to kiss him again.

Maybe more than that.

She knew what was happening here. Alex was a temporary diversion. She was feeling anxiety over the reality that they were close to finding Carter. Alex was no doubt feeling the same anxiety.

Crossing her arms over her chest, she moved toward the edge of the pool. Maybe what she needed to do was jump in and cool off.

She looked over her shoulder at Alex. And then he advanced, and all rational excuses for her attraction to him fled her mind.

"One kiss won't do," he said, pulling her into his arms. "Not hardly."

He brushed his lips over hers, deliberately holding back from kissing her deeply. He wanted to see her reaction.

To feel it.

Beneath his mouth, he felt hers quiver.

Alex eased back and stared down at her. Her eyes as wide as plates as she looked at him, a mix of confusion and desire swirling in their depths. She'd wanted him to give her a passionate kiss.

Oh, yes. There was most definitely mutual attraction.

Lowering his face to hers again, Alex ended both of their suffering. He captured her lips with his.

For a few seconds, Brianne didn't move. She didn't kiss him back, nor did she pull away. Just when Alex was about to pull back, wondering if he'd mistaken her desire after all, Brianne's mouth opened beneath his and she emitted a soft moan.

The sound may have been faint, but to Alex, it was like a roar of passion. He wrapped his arms around her and deepened the kiss, enjoying the feel of her full lips and the delicious taste of her tongue.

Another moan, and Alex's body erupted

in heat. She wanted him. Just as he wanted her.

Abruptly, she jerked away from him. She stumbled backward, almost falling into the pool. Alex grabbed her by the shoulder and pulled her toward him, stopping her before she fell in.

Her breasts pressed against his chest. Three seconds passed. Then Brianne stepped away from him again, this time making sure to step away from the pool.

But Alex wasn't ready to let her go. Reaching out, he snagged her wrist. "Brianne —"

She looked at him, her expression stunned. For several seconds, neither of them said a word. Then Brianne said, "Why do you keep doing that? Why do you keep kissing me?"

She sounded breathless and sexy as hell. Alex wanted to take her in his arms and carry her into the house, take off that bikini that had been driving him crazy and make sweet love to her.

Maybe it was the comment he was sure she had muttered, that she wasn't sure she wanted things to be the same with Carter again. Or maybe it was simply the reality that being this close to her day in and day out, made it too hard to resist touching her. It was as if she had some sort of spell on him she refused to break.

He'd been doing his best to avoid her, but hadn't this moment been inevitable? He loved the way her smile lit up her whole face, and the sound of her soft laugh. And her eyes . . . She gazed at him as if trying to see into his soul. Had Alex read more into those looks than Brianne had intended?

"Why?" she asked again.

"I could ask you the same thing."

Brianne's eyes grew wide with indignation. "Excuse me?"

"You kissed me back."

Her back grew instantly stiff, and she pulled the towel tighter around her. She was closing herself off from him. "I did not."

"You didn't?"

Brianne marched past Alex toward the patio door.

Running scared.

The thought made him smile, because it proved to him that his feeling were *not* one-sided.

He followed her. Brianne either heard or sensed him, because she glanced over her shoulder and said, "I'm going up to the bedroom."

Alex would never know what had gotten into him, but he found himself saying, "You want me to join you?"

Brianne spun around, her eyes flashing fire as she faced him. Alex held her gaze, not backing down. He wanted her to know the invitation was serious. Maybe falling into bed would relieve the tension they were both feeling.

Brianne didn't respond. She simply whirled back around and scurried toward the foyer.

Alex let her leave. His heart was pounding, but inwardly he was smiling.

Brianne *had* kissed him back.

Sure, she'd ultimately ended the kiss and gone cold, but for several glorious seconds, she had been his.

And Alex was determined that she would be his again.

CHAPTER 12

For a full hour, Brianne lay on her bed beneath the covers, tossing and turning and huffing.

You kissed me back.

The nerve!

Alex had wrapped his arms around her. *Alex* had lowered his mouth to hers. *Alex* was the one who started kissing *her.*

Those were indisputable facts. And yet he dared to try to put the blame on her for what had happened.

You kissed me back.

Brianne turned onto her back, kicking her legs harshly to free them from the bed sheets. She groaned in frustration — and then realized it wasn't the sheets she was frustrated with.

She was frustrated with herself.

Because Alex had been right. She *had* kissed him back.

But only because he had dared to kiss her

first. He had to take the blame for this.

Brianne found herself wondering why she was trying to assign blame so badly. A kiss wasn't the worst thing in the world. And at least she had been the one to stop it.

The answer came to her almost immediately. She wanted to assign blame because she'd *enjoyed* the kiss.

As the thought came to her, she relaxed her rigid body and allowed herself to remember the feel of Alex's lips against hers. They had been soft and moved with skill, igniting heat in her body she hadn't felt for a long time.

In over three years.

She sighed, savoring the memory of the kiss and the way it had electrified every cell in her body. For those moments while she'd been lost in Alex and his undeniable sex appeal, they had been the only two people in the world.

What was she doing? Why was she even remembering the kiss with fondness? She was here to find Carter, not fall into bed with his best friend.

Her anger returned, and she embraced it.

She didn't have the right to enjoy Alex's kiss. Clearly, she was suffering some sort of delusion. Perhaps some kind of transference of affection — she was certain there was a medical name for it. Alex had been Carter's closest friend, and she was somehow seeing Carter in Alex.

Relief washed over her with that thought. Yes, that made sense. It was the *only* thing that made sense.

But despite Brianne's conclusion, when she fell into a nap, the person she dreamed about was Alex, not Carter.

Later, when there was a knock on her door, Brianne bolted upright in bed. Then she grabbed the sheets and held them over her chest. She was still in her bathing suit.

Not that Alex hadn't already had an unobstructed view of her in the suit. Was there really a need to cover up?

"Brianne?" Alex called. "Can I come in?"

"Sure," she said.

The door opened, and Brianne knew immediately that something was seriously wrong with her. Because seeing Alex, covered up in a T-shirt and athletic pants — made her heart accelerate. Lord, the man was *fine*.

Alex's eyes registered surprise. No doubt, he was shocked to see her in bed. "I fell asleep," Brianne explained.

"I was thinking we could head out to get a bite to eat. If you're up to it."

"I . . ." Brianne wanted to say no, but not because she wasn't hungry. In fact, she could probably devour an entire chocolate cake. She wanted to keep her distance from Alex, even though she knew that wasn't realistic.

Alex stepped into the room, and Brianne held the sheet tighter to her chest. "Brianne, I'm not going to attack you."

She suddenly felt foolish. But she said, "Are you sure about that?"

"You want me to apologize for kissing you?"

No. Not really. "Yes."

"Okay, then. I'm sorry. I think . . . we're both a little . . . stressed."

Though she had asked for it, Alex's apology left her feeling empty. It bothered her to think that for him the kiss had simply been a reaction to stress.

"No word from Dean's friend?"

"Nothing."

"And Ginny?" Brianne asked, wondering why that question had come from her mouth.

"Yeah, she called."

Brianne's heart deflated.

"She wanted to tell me that she was going to try to do a little digging, see what she could find out."

176

I'll bet. "Well, that's good," Brianne said, hoping she didn't sound irritated. The truth was, if Alex got involved with Ginny it would be good for her. He wouldn't be tempted to try and lay any more kisses on her.

You kissed me back.

"I'll get dressed," Brianne said. "See you downstairs in a bit."

Alex nodded and then left the room.

Brianne was craving a triple cheeseburger smothered with mayonnaise and ketchup, with a large side of seasoned fries. But she was determined not to binge on food. She'd been doing such a great job at sticking to a healthy diet and wasn't about to let her stress over a silly meaningless kiss be her undoing.

It was after three and still sunny outside, but Brianne dressed in a long-sleeve mock turtleneck and jeans. She combed her short hair, not caring that she hadn't straightened it. And she didn't bother applying any makeup.

It's not like she was trying to impress anyone.

As she checked out her reflection, she couldn't help thinking that she was trying too hard to show that she was inaccessible.

Ready, she retrieved her purse and headed

downstairs. Alex was sitting on the wrought-iron bench in the foyer. Seeing him, Brianne's breath snagged in her throat. He had changed, too. While she had gone for the "cover me up so I don't look like I'm flirting" look, Alex had done just the opposite. He was wearing a body-hugging white T-shirt that showcased his rippling stomach muscles and bulging arms. His jeans were slung low on his hips in a look that screamed sexy without the effort.

No man had the right to look that good.

His eyes swept over her quickly — nothing overt, like the way she'd noticed him checking her out earlier in her bikini — but still she felt heat. Maybe she was coming down with something.

Yeah, I'm losing my mind.

"You ready?" Alex asked.

Brianne suddenly wasn't sure that she was. She had hoped that a few hours of reflection would help her rid herself of any thoughts about Alex. Instead, seeing him again oozing sex appeal, she couldn't help feeling that she would like *him* for an early dinner.

"You're dressed kind of warmly," Alex said as she stepped onto the main level. "This isn't Buffalo."

"I don't mind being a bit warm." Not a

total lie, but not the reason she was wearing a turtleneck. She didn't look at Alex, just made her way to the door, hoping he wouldn't point out the hypocrisy in her statement. Earlier today, she'd been prancing around in a bikini. Now she was dressed as if she expected chilly temperatures in Daytona.

The moment she stepped outside, she knew she was overdressed. The sun hung high in the sky, still providing incredible warmth. While it was November and not nearly as hot as in the summer, her top was still overkill for the warm Daytona weather. Beside Alex in his short sleeves, Brianne looked ridiculous.

Just the short walk to the car and she was starting to sweat.

Inside the vehicle, she turned the air-conditioning control on her side of the car on high.

"If you want to change . . ."

"No, I'm fine. I expect the restaurant to be pretty cold, so I'm good."

"Suit yourself," Alex mumbled.

Brianne didn't respond. Nor did she look at him.

"Any idea what you want to eat?" Alex asked.

"Actually, I wouldn't mind pancakes,"

Brianne said. She needed something sweet. Not too much. She wouldn't binge. But she hoped that eating something sweet would satisfy the undeniable craving she had for Alex Thorpe.

"There's a pancake house on the main strip. They serve breakfast all day."

"Sounds good."

Alex eyed Brianne surreptitiously as he steered the car out of his driveway. She sat with her back ramrod straight and her gaze straight ahead, as if she feared that by looking at him she would turn to stone. Actually, she was doing a very good impression of a stone sculpture as it was. . . .

"Are you planning to talk to me again?" he asked.

"Of course I am," Brianne said, her gaze still straight ahead.

"Then are you ever planning to look at me again?"

"I —" She stopped abruptly. Slowly, she faced him — but she didn't hold his gaze for more than a beat. "There. I looked at you."

"Do I make you uncomfortable?" Alex asked.

Brianne's mouth fell open, but whatever she was about to say, she thought better of. Instead she paused, inhaled a deep breath, then spoke. "You're being a tad overdramatic, don't ya think?"

"Before I kissed you, you didn't have a problem making eye contact. Now it's like you're afraid if you look at me you'll be struck by lightning."

"Definitely being overdramatic," she said and forced a laugh. But she still didn't meet his gaze.

Alex had apologized for kissing her, more as a way to put her at ease. But now he was getting a pretty good idea that the kiss had affected her far more than she likely wanted to admit.

He pulled the car to the side of the road and killed the engine. Now Brianne faced him. "What are you doing?"

"Stopping the car so we can talk."

"Oh, for crying out loud."

Now Brianne sounded angry. "What is your problem?" Alex asked. "Is it because I kissed you?"

"You think that kiss changed my world? Well, it didn't."

The words hurt. "Then why do you suddenly seem so angry with me?"

"There's nothing sudden about it," Brianne retorted.

Alex stared at her in disbelief. "What?"

Brianne's chest was heaving. She *was*

angry, and she didn't really know why. She only knew that calling on the anger was all she had right now to keep her from thinking about the thoughts she'd been having regarding Alex since he had kissed her earlier.

"You want the truth? I am angry with you. I have been for a long time."

"Ah, so you want to have it out with me. All right then. Go ahead. Have at it."

"Okay," Brianne said, and paused. "Sure we're here now trying to find Carter and right a wrong, but if it hadn't been for you, he might never have gone missing in the first place."

"*What?* You blame me for Carter going missing?"

"Yes, I blame you," she snapped, frustrated. "You were the one he always ran off with on those crazy adventures. Base jumping off of mountains and buildings. Extreme skiing. I mean, who in their right mind goes extreme skiing? Who would put themselves in harm's way when they've got a loved one waiting at home? Oh, yeah. Carter. And you."

"And you blame me for that?"

"You knew how much I hated all of your crazy extreme sports, yet you never said, 'Gosh, Carter is engaged now, maybe we shouldn't do this.' "

"You think I could have stopped Carter? He was a big boy and would have done whatever he wanted, with or without me."

"Then it should have been without you. You enabled him."

Alex nodded slowly, acknowledging that he heard her comment. And Brianne felt a smidgen of guilt. The truth was, she couldn't truly blame Alex. It simply felt good to unleash her emotions via anger — instead of kissing him senseless.

"What happened that day?" Brianne asked. "That day on the mountain? How did you and Carter get separated?"

"We just did, Brianne," Alex answered. "I was looking for wood, and he went ahead, and the next thing I knew the snow was coming down heavily and I couldn't find him."

It was the same answer Alex had given her before, but like the other times she had heard it, Brianne didn't believe him. He was keeping something from her — that much she knew. But what?

"You think it doesn't eat me up that I got off the mountain alive and Carter didn't?" Alex asked. "I was racked with guilt — until the day I saw him on television."

"So racked with guilt that you gave up on him."

"What do you mean?"

"The police called off the search and you just accepted that we'd never find him again," Brianne explained. "Maybe if you hadn't given up on him, we wouldn't be here right now."

Alex's jaw tightened, and Brianne instantly regretted her words. "I'm sorry," she quickly said. "That wasn't fair."

"No, I can see why you feel that way. But what you don't know is that I didn't give up on Carter. The authorities called off the search, but I hired a team of searchers to comb the mountains after that. Before that first memorial, actually. Then again, three months later when the weather had gotten better."

Brianne's lips parted in surprise. "You . . . you never said anything."

"You weren't exactly happy to talk to me on the occasions we were in touch. Besides, I had no news."

"Alex, I'm sorry. I just went off on you like you never cared for Carter, and that was so wrong of me. Please forgive me."

Alex started the car again. "Don't sweat it. We're both stressed. The situation is getting to both of us."

"Yeah," Brianne said softly. "You're right."

They drove the rest of the way to the pancake house in silence. Every time Brianne glanced at Alex, his eyes were on the road.

He was probably upset with her. And she wouldn't blame him. Though she had been mad at him in the past, she wasn't currently mad at him for any of the reasons she had spewed.

In fact, she wasn't mad at him at all.

She was mad at herself.

Mad that she seemed powerless to fight the undeniable attraction she was feeling for Alex.

Why was she having these feelings now? At a time when there was finally hope of her greatest wish coming true?

Because if things went as planned, she would be reunited with Carter in a few days.

So she had better get over whatever it was she was feeling for Alex.

And fast.

CHAPTER 13

What happened on the mountain?

It was a question Brianne had asked him more than once, and more than once he had lied to her.

He had lied to her to protect her. How could he tell her a truth he knew would crush her? At least at the time, when she'd been so utterly fragile?

As Alex lay on the bed in his room, his mind went back to that fateful day in British Columbia. It was right about then that he had started to see that the man he'd considered his best friend had a heart of stone. He had been gloating about the fact that he was seeing another woman, one of Brianne's friends who had moved to Florida. Carter had already been making a plan to see this other woman when they got back home and wanted Alex's cooperation in creating a cover story he could spoon-feed Brianne.

"What the hell are you doing?" Alex had asked. "You're engaged, bro. Why are you stringing some other woman along?"

"Who says I'm stringing her along?"

"You're getting married, right?"

"That doesn't mean I can't have a little something on the side," Carter had said, playfully elbowing Alex.

Instead of joining his friend in a laugh about something that wasn't in the least bit funny, Alex had gotten mad. "Are you serious?"

"Hell yeah, I'm serious."

"Do you love Brianne or not?"

"Brianne will make a great wife. A great mother. But a guy needs a woman who can take a walk on the wild side. Satisfy his other needs, ya know?"

Alex's blood began to boil. "So you're gonna marry her and not even plan to be faithful to her?"

"What's the big deal?"

"The big deal is you're being a big jerk. Brianne doesn't deserve that. She loves you. God only knows why."

"What was that?"

"You heard me," Alex spat out. "Do the right thing. Either dump this other woman, or dump Brianne."

"Or what?"

Alex didn't answer. He was done speaking on the subject. He started marching past Carter on the trail.

Only Carter grabbed him by his parka and whirled him around. "You've still got a thing for her, don't you?"

Alex said nothing.

"You're acting all high and mighty, but the real deal is you're jealous. You wanted a piece of her, but I got to her first."

"I did not want a *piece* of her."

Carter laughed in his face. "Yeah, right. I bet it's killing you. This one chose me."

"You're still harping on that girl from two years ago?" A couple of years earlier, a woman Carter had been interested in had made a play for Alex. He'd shot her down — and told Carter the deal.

"She was trash," Carter said.

"And Brianne isn't. So do right by her. If that means letting her down easy —"

"So you can have my sloppy seconds?"

Alex couldn't help himself. He punched Carter in the face. His friend's head jerked backward, and he stumbled. But when Carter caught his footing and stood upright again, Alex had seen the blood pouring from his nose.

"You son of a —" Carter had spit out.

"Don't hurt her," Alex had warned. "Because if you do, you'll have to answer to me."

Then he had turned and stalked away from Carter, leaving him on the mountain as the snow had begun to fall.

In the years following Carter's disappearance, the memory of what had happened on the mountain had filled Alex with guilt. Now, it filled him with anger.

Because if Carter was alive, he had orchestrated the kind of deception that devastated lives.

He'd meant what he'd said to Carter that day. If he hurt Brianne, he would have to answer to him.

And that was exactly what would happen when they found Carter. For the years of suffering, and for the theft of the ring that Alex's mother had given to him, Carter would have to answer to him.

And if Carter thought he had seen an ugly side of Alex that day on the mountain, he hadn't seen anything yet.

The next morning, after Alex's run on the beach and his shower in the outdoor facility, he entered the house to find Brianne in the gym. She was furiously peddling away on his stationary bike and didn't notice him come in. But after a moment, she caught his reflection in the mirror, and her peddling slowed.

"Don't stop on account of me," Alex said. "I just came to say good morning."

Brianne slowed to a stop. "I was finishing up anyway."

"You sure?"

"Yeah." A beat. "Any news?"

"I just checked my voice mail and there were no messages from Dean's friend," Alex answered. "Either he can't be reached where he is overseas, or the guy might not be willing to call us back. Regardless, I don't want to sit around waiting for a call that might come in a few days, or never."

"What should we do? Call Dean again?"

"Actually, I'm thinking maybe we should go to the police."

"The police?" Brianne asked, surprised. She climbed off the bike.

"It's a long shot, but Dean's guarded reaction got me thinking. What if Carter was ever in trouble with the law? Maybe they know who he is. I don't know. Maybe it's a crazy idea."

Brianne shrugged. "I guess it can't hurt."

"Ah, maybe I shouldn't jump the gun. We can certainly wait another day to hear from Dean's friend. And then there's Ginny. She might find some info for me."

"Right. Ginny."

Brianne spoke the woman's name as if she had some sort of gripe with her. What gripe could she have, other than jealousy?

It was a nice thought, that Brianne was jealous. Because it meant she cared. More than she wanted to admit.

"You want to take a dip with me in the pool?" Alex asked. "Maybe use the sauna?"

"No, I'm good. I'm just gonna hit the shower."

Brianne walked past him out of the gym. Alex wanted to follow her, but he didn't. She had already become more distant since their kiss the day before, and he didn't want to risk pushing her away altogether. If she needed space, he'd give her space.

While Brianne showered, Alex prepared breakfast. When he'd spent some time in France, he had learned how to make the best crepes. It was a fine art he had mastered, and he was certain Brianne would love them.

Brianne came down the stairs about twenty minutes later, pausing when she stepped into the kitchen and saw the food on the table. She was wearing another ridiculous long-sleeve shirt and no makeup — as if that would render her undesirable. If anything, it made it clear just how much of a natural beauty she was.

"You made breakfast?"

"It was my turn."

She inhaled the alluring scent of the food. "Are those crepes?"

"Strawberry crepes. I hope you like them."

"Like them? I love them." Brianne pulled out a chair and sat at the table. "You made these from scratch?"

"Yep." Alex brought the coffee carafe and two large mugs to the table. "I learned to make them in Paris."

"Paris?" Something flickered in her eyes. "Did you spend time there with that model girlfriend you mentioned? Catilla?"

"Catarina."

"Whatever."

A smile played on Alex's lips. "You sound jealous."

"Jealous?" she scoffed. "Not hardly. There was only one time I was ever jealous, and that was when I thought a friend of mine was making a play for Carter."

"A friend of yours?" Alex asked, suddenly intrigued. It had to be Carter's other woman. The woman's name that he'd forgotten.

"A former friend," Brianne explained. "Tracy. I had to drop her when she wouldn't stop cooing and cawing over Carter. The few times she hung out with me and him, she was so flirty, as if she wanted to steal my man."

"Really?"

"She worked in a hotel and was transferred to another location," Brianne went on. "I don't know where."

Right here, Brianne. She moved to Daytona.

Alex didn't dare say that. Instead he urged, "Go on. Take a bite."

Brianne did. The expression on her face said she'd died and gone to heaven. "Alex, this is *delicious!* Light and fluffy. I don't know if I've tasted anything better."

"I'm glad you approve."

As Alex watched her eat, it struck him that he could really get used to spending each day with her like this. Just the two of them, secluded from the outside world, enjoying domestic life.

At home, Alex was always on the go. When he made breakfast, he typically ate it standing at the counter. It would be nice to sit down at a table every day, have a conversation over a meal. Share a dessert.

Then make hot, passionate love on the counter . . .

"Did you hear me?" Brianne asked.

Brianne's words shook him from his fantasy, and Alex had to clear his throat before speaking. "No, sorry. What were you saying?"

"Just that I was thinking that Carter might not even be in Daytona. People travel from all over the country to attend the Fall Cycle Scene. Honestly, he could be from anywhere."

"He's here," Alex said, with no room for doubt.

"How can you be sure?"

"Just . . . a feeling," Alex answered. Daytona was a piece of the puzzle he had missed, given that he'd believed Carter had died. But it was a place he and Carter had scoped for a potential storefront — and the place where Carter's girlfriend lived.

"Well, I guess it can't hurt to do the best search we can here. If we don't hear from Dean today, maybe we should put up posters with Carter's picture. Someone may know him, see the poster and contact us. In addition to going to the police. We need to do whatever we can to find him as quickly as possible."

Alex felt oddly perturbed at her words. She wanted to find Carter as quickly as possible. But he wasn't quite ready to find his former friend. He wanted to spend as much time with Brianne as possible before having to break the truth to her.

"Hopefully we'll get some answers today," Alex said.

"Yes, hopefully. Before we . . ."

Her eyes widening, her voice trailed off. She looked like she had been surprised by the words that had come from her mouth.

"Before we what?" Alex asked.

She ate another piece of her crepe.

Alex wasn't about to let the unfinished comment slide. "Before we what?" he pressed.

"Slip of the tongue," Brianne responded, not looking at him.

He wanted to slip his tongue into her mouth. "You're afraid something is going to happen between us again."

"*Nothing* happened between us," Brianne clarified.

Alex hesitated a beat. "I beg to differ."

Brianne reached for the carafe. "You can't even look at me," Alex said.

She put the carafe down. "Why are you doing this?"

Why was he? He knew why. Because he wanted to explore what Brianne was feeling for him *before* they found Carter. Before Carter had a chance to sweet-talk her, play on her emotions and appeal to her sense of loyalty.

"What if I told you that Ginny called and

asked me out?"

Brianne's eyes widened. "Did she?"

"The very idea bothers you," Alex said.

She filled her coffee mug. "It does not."

"It does. It bothers you that I might go out with Ginny. You don't like thinking of me and Catarina together. Why's that?"

"You are delusional. I'm in love with Carter, remember? You can sleep with all the models in the world, I don't care."

Alex was actually amused. It didn't take a trained therapist to see that Brianne was lying through her teeth. She was doing everything in her power to deny that she felt anything for him.

And once again she was covered up in a long-sleeve shirt. Not quite as bad as the turtleneck she'd donned yesterday, but he would bet his last dollar that her motive was to appear less attractive.

To him.

"Why are you smiling?" Brianne suddenly asked, her tone accusatory.

"Excuse me?"

"That — that smirk on your face. What's so funny?"

"It's a beautiful day. Can't I smile?"

She put down her fork, and it clattered against the plate. "It's very obvious that despite what you said about us both being stressed, you're trying to read more into that . . . that kiss. It meant nothing. At best, it was a . . . a gesture of comfort."

"Comfort?"

"Yes, comfort."

"If that's what you need to believe."

Brianne gaped at him. Why was he pushing the issue? Didn't he realize that she was consumed with guilt over kissing her fiancé's best friend?

"Maybe this was a mistake," she said.

"What? Eating breakfast with me?"

"No, coming here with you. To Daytona." She glanced at the backyard, her chest heaving. "I don't even understand why you're trying to make a big deal out of the kiss. You never even liked me. Why would you even try to act like a kiss between us would mean something?"

One of Alex's eyebrows shot up. "I never liked you?"

"You know you didn't," Brianne said. "You barely tolerated me when I was dating Carter."

Alex actually chuckled. "You couldn't be more wrong."

Brianne scoffed. "Now you want to change history?"

Change history? Was she serious? "Why would you ever say that I didn't like you?"

"Because you did your best to avoid me like the plague," Brianne said. "I'd come into the store to see Carter, and you would barely utter a hello. I know I wasn't gorgeous or thin like the women you typically date, but I thought you would accept me because I loved Carter."

If Brianne had just told Alex that she had shot someone in cold blood, he would have been less surprised. "You think I didn't like you because you weren't gorgeous or thin?"

Brianne gave Alex a defiant look, challenging him to deny her accusation.

"That's insane," Alex said. "I always liked you." When Brianne rolled her eyes, Alex shot out of his chair and rounded the table until he was standing in front of her. He braced his hands on both sides of the chair's arm rests and stared into her eyes. "And I always thought you were gorgeous. Do you forget me telling you that I always thought you were beautiful — even when you weren't as thin as now? In fact, I distinctly remember telling you that I liked the curves you had back then. Do you want me to kiss you again to prove just how much I've always liked you?"

Brianne said nothing, but Alex could see the rise and fall of her chest. The startled yet wild look in her eyes. He also saw the way her bottom lip quivered and *knew* that she did want him to kiss her again. Oh, she might pretend that she didn't, but Alex was past the point of pretending.

So he curled his hand around her neck and pulled her toward him while lowering his face to hers. Their lips met in a fury of passion. This time, Brianne didn't hold back, taking her time to warm to the kiss. She opened her mouth wide, allowing his tongue total access.

Alex flicked his tongue over hers, nipped at her bottom lip, then suckled the tip of her tongue.

Brianne purred, and it was Alex's undoing. He slipped his other hand around her waist and pulled her to her feet. He crushed her body against his, kissing her with the kind of fervor that said he had waited far too long to do this.

Brianne curled her arms around his neck. Alex slipped his hands beneath the hem of her shirt and moved them up over her hips slowly, enjoying every inch of her delectable curves. When his palms reached her waist, Brianne shuddered.

Alex raised his hands, moving them along her heated skin until he reached the curve of her breasts. A groan tore from his throat.

He wanted all of her. Now. One hell of a

kiss simply wasn't enough.

Tearing his lips from hers, he brought his mouth to the underside of her jaw, using his tongue to tease her soft skin. While his tongue flicked over her flesh, his thumbs flicked over her nipples.

Brianne's body went boneless. If she didn't have her arms secured around Alex's neck, she was certain she would collapse in a heap on the floor. His fingers and mouth were driving her crazy.

Far more crazy than Carter's ever had.

Carter . . . The moment she thought about him, her body went stiff. *What am I doing? What am I doing?*

She jerked backward, away from Alex's touch. His eyes were heavy-lidded and smoky, radiating raw desire.

Brianne brought a hand to her mouth, touching her swollen lips. "Alex . . ."

"You are beautiful and sexy," Alex said, his voice husky. "But besides that fact, I always liked that you were grounded. You're a real woman. Caring and thoughtful and genuine."

"But . . . but you never liked me. Even Carter noticed."

"Carter noticed?" Alex said, and Brianne was certain that his voice was tinged with anger.

"He even said that you told him you thought I was flighty."

Brianne gasped when Alex snared his arm around her waist and pulled her against him. He kissed her again, deep and hot. When he pulled away, Brianne was actually disappointed.

"Don't believe what Carter told you. You were the perfect woman for him, and he didn't —"

An alarm bell went off in Brianne's brain. She narrowed her eyes as she looked at Alex. "Didn't what? What were you about to say?"

"Didn't appreciate your beauty," Alex finished. "The fact that he wanted you to lose weight . . ."

"Oh." Brianne was certain he'd been about to say something else.

"If you thought I didn't like you, maybe it's because my best friend was dating you. Carter could be territorial. He had a bit of a jealous streak. His mother cheated on his father, and he never got over it. I was always aware that if you and I were too chummy, it might have made Carter doubt your affections."

Brianne stared at Alex in surprise. Several seconds passed before she spoke. "Carter's mother had an affair?"

"Yeah. He didn't tell you?"

Brianne shook her head. "He never mentioned it. And I can't imagine why. I thought he told me everything."

Though the truth was, she had often sensed that there were things Carter was holding back. She would gently try to coax his feelings out of him, but she could tell he was never sharing his deepest feelings with her. She had noticed the disconnect more and more in the days before he'd left for British Columbia and had wondered if she'd done something to push him away.

"I don't want to talk about Carter anymore," Alex said and emitted a shuddery breath. "I want to talk about what's happening between us."

Brianne took a step backward.

"No. Don't do that. Don't step away from me."

"All right." Brianne stopped, gulped in air. "I'm not going to deny that there's . . . an attraction." How could she, when her body was still thrumming from his touch? "But Alex, I'm here with you because we're trying to find Carter. My *fiancé.*"

"Former fiancé."

"Why are you doing this?" Her heart thundered. "Why now?"

Alex's cell phone rang, and both of them

started. The trilling phone instantly marred the moment between them.

"Dean's friend," Brianne guessed.

Alex made his way to the living room and quickly scooped up his phone. He glanced at the caller ID and then threw a look at Brianne and nodded.

"Bingo," Alex said. "It's Dean's number."

CHAPTER 14

Brianne should have seen the call as a relief. As something that thankfully broke the intense sexual tension between her and Alex. And yet, oddly, she was a little unhappy about the distraction.

"He doesn't want to talk to me?" Alex was saying.

Wrapping her arms around her torso, Brianne slowly made her way toward Alex.

"I really can't get into it. All I can say is that it's a personal matter. If your friend's willing to call me, I can —"

Brianne stood behind Alex. She couldn't help dropping her eyes to his behind, which looked oh-so-good in his jeans. Why was it that he had made her body come alive in a way that the man she'd been engaged to marry hadn't? What was it about him?

"Actually, please tell him not to mention my name. Yeah, I know that sounds sketchy.

You just have to trust that I have my reasons."

His shoulders. His back. And, oh, those
thighs. Brianne felt a hot flush just looking
at him.

"Damn," Alex muttered and lowered the
phone from his ear.

"Bad news?" she asked.

"It sounds like Dean's friend is wary. He
doesn't even want to talk to me."

"He won't even call?"

Alex shook his head. "Which only makes
me think that Carter must be in some kind
of trouble. His friends are protecting him
like they think someone wants to do him
harm."

"Why don't you just tell him who we are
and why we're here?"

Alex didn't answer, just made a face and
walked toward the living room's floor-to-
ceiling windows.

"Why not, Alex?" Brianne asked, following him. "Being all secretive is only making
Dean suspicious. But if you tell him about
your trip to the Rockies with Carter, how
he got lost and somehow ended up in Daytona, surely they'll understand."

"I don't know about that."

"I really don't think going to the police is
going to help. Carter's going by the name

Donnie. They won't know who he is if they don't have his full name."

"Hmm. You could be right about that."

"So tell Dean the deal."

When Alex didn't answer, Brianne eased her body between him and the window. "Don't I get a say? You wanted me along to help you. We're supposed to be working together. At what point am I allowed to contribute my ideas?"

"I just need a moment, Brianne."

She frowned. "What is this? Did you lure me down here under false pretenses? To what, get me into bed or something?"

"Wow. You really just said that."

"What am I supposed to think right now? If you tell Dean exactly who we are and why we want to find Carter, he'll realize we're not a threat. If you don't want to do that, then I have to think you had some other motive for bringing me down here."

"Maybe my motive is to protect you."

"Protect me?" Brianne stared at Alex, but his expression gave nothing away. "Alex, I'm not really sure what's going on here. But let's get on with this already. You talked about Carter having issues of trust because his mother had an affair. Maybe there's a psychological reason for his amnesia. Maybe he's running from his pain. In which case he needs us more than ever. He needs someone to nurture and love him back to emotional health."

"Are you serious?" There was an edge to Alex's voice.

"Yes, I'm serious. Maybe Carter was always going off on some adventure as a coping mechanism. He was avoiding dealing with his past the way a person turns to alcohol to avoid dealing with their emotions."

Alex rolled his eyes.

"See! What's that about? You're rolling your eyes. Suddenly I'm starting to feel that you're not here to find Carter because you're his friend, but for another reason. I'm a big girl. Tell me if there's something else going on."

"You want to know the truth?" Alex asked, sounding exasperated.

"Yes, I want to know the truth."

"All right, then. You're going to find out soon enough."

Brianne's heart slammed against her chest. Alex's tone suddenly had her scared.

"Carter lied to you, Brianne." This wasn't the way Alex had envisioned telling her about Carter, but maybe it was time. Because since Dean's friend wasn't cooperating, it was time for Plan B. And he was tired of the lying, the pretending that they were on the hunt for a friend who was suffering some kind of memory loss. He hadn't expected that lying to Brianne would bother him so much, mainly because he'd been focused on his goal. But seeing how she was suddenly focusing on Carter's emotional issues and concocting another reason for his memory loss, how she was clinging to the fairy tale that they would pick up the pieces and sail off into the sunset . . . Well, no more.

"Carter isn't this helpless victim of emotional trauma that you're making him out to be. In fact, I'm starting to think he was a very skilled liar."

Brianne's mouth fell open as she stared at Alex. First, she looked baffled. But then her expression became defiant. "I see what you're doing."

"What am I doing?"

She stepped away from him. "Suddenly you're bashing him, calling him a liar."

"He is a liar. He was."

"Yeah, now that you've decided you're attracted to me. Yes, I kissed you. Yes, there was a spark of something. So now you want to turn me against Carter before we find him again!"

"That is not true."

Brianne shook her head back and forth, the expression on her face cutting him like a knife. "I . . . I'm leaving."

She marched away, but Alex was right on her heel. "Brianne —"

"No, Alex. I've had enough of this. If you don't want to find Carter, fine. But I'm going to Dean and —"

Alex grabbed her by the arm and whirled her around. "I assure you, I am not trying to badmouth Carter as a ploy to win you over. That's not who I am. That's not what I'm about. But there are some things about Carter . . . some things I know, some things I suspected. All of it I should have told you about before we came down here."

Brianne whimpered. "I want cake."

"What?"

"Or chocolate. Or both." Gone was her defiance. She looked vulnerable and sad.

"Brianne." Alex pulled her into his arms. She shrugged out of his embrace. "No. Don't."

"Why don't we sit down?" Alex said gently.

"Just tell me."

"Let's sit."

A tear fell down her cheek. "Is the news going to be better if I'm sitting?"

Heck, this wasn't how Alex had planned to tell her. Truthfully, he hadn't had a plan.

He should have known it would be like this, with Brianne in tears and him feeling like a world-class jerk.

"You mentioned your friend Tracy earlier. That she always flirted with Carter. That you felt she secretly wanted to steal your man." Alex paused, hoping to let his words register. But Brianne just stared up at him, still confused, still hurt. "Well, you were right, Brianne. Tracy did have a thing for Carter. And he . . . he had a thing for her."

The seconds that passed seemed like hours, as Alex's words registered. He saw every muscle in Brianne's face collapse.

"No."

"Brianne, I wish it wasn't true. When I found out, I tried to make Carter see reason."

"No!"

"I wouldn't mention it if it didn't fit in with my theory of what's going on now."

Brianne looked so lost, Alex wasn't sure she'd even heard him. She went limp and began to collapse. Alex reached out and caught her before she fell to the floor. This was why he'd wanted her sitting down.

"No . . . no . . ." She pounded his chest.

"I'm sorry, Brianne."

"He was sleeping with her?"

There was no sugar coating this. "Yes."

"After we got engaged?"

"Yes."

Brianne began to cry. Alex held her, even as she twisted in his arms. He comforted her while she cried, alternately clinging to him and trying to free herself of him.

After a few minutes, she looked up at him. "But how? When? Tracy had moved away before we got engaged."

Brianne abruptly stopped. She stiffened in Alex's arms as she looked up at him in horror. She understood now. Finally.

She shook her head. "No. Alex, please. No."

Alex led her to the sofa. "Brianne, take a seat."

"No!" She shook out of Alex's arms. "Tell me the truth, and tell me right now. Tracy moved to Daytona, didn't she? You — you think he's *living* with her!"

Alex said nothing.

"But that would mean he . . ." Her voice trailed off as pain streaked across her face. "He faked his death? He . . . he left me for her?"

"Please, Brianne. Sit."

"And you knew." She shot him an accusing glare. "You *knew*."

"I didn't know, Brianne. But when I saw him on television, in Daytona, I began to suspect. All these years, I thought he was dead —"

"But you knew he was involved with Tracy!"

That Alex couldn't deny. "Yes," he admitted quietly.

"And you never told me. You — you were going to let me marry him."

"I tried to talk him out of what he was doing. I told him that living a double life wasn't fair to you. Even the last day I saw him, I told him that he needed to stop what he was doing and be honest with you. That was the last conversation we had on the mountain."

Brianne gasped and gripped her belly. "Oh, my God."

"Brianne, sit."

"No!" She shouted the word, her chest heaving. Alex didn't know what to do to comfort her, to ease her pain. She looked like she was going to fall apart.

And then she looked at him again, as if she'd just had another revelation. "Wait a minute. What do you mean double life? Cheating is cheating, but a double life . . ."

"Brianne, I'll tell you everything. I just want you to sit down. I want to have a calm chat about the facts."

"How can we have a calm chat about Carter playing me for a fool?"

Alex stared at her, several beats passing. There was no doubt that she was crushed. But seeing her so devastated was like a kick in the gut. Especially after the explosive passion between them earlier.

"Three years have passed, Brianne," Alex began carefully. "Are you honestly this devastated?"

Brianne's eyes flashed fire, and for a moment Alex thought she might slap him. "How dare you. How *dare* you!"

"Okay, that came out wrong. I just mean . . . it's not like this is a fresh wound. All this happened in the past."

"I hate you," she snapped.

The words cut him. Cut him deep. "Brianne —"

"I mean it, Alex. You're too self-absorbed to realize that this isn't about the past. It's about the present. Right now. The fact that *you* lied to me about Carter. You had me come down here with you under false pretenses, acting like we were on a mission to find a man who had likely lost his memory."

"That was your theory —"

"But you went along with it! You never once said that I was off base. Way off base."

"It's not that simple."

"It is that simple. You tell the truth, or you lie. You chose to lie to me."

Alex dragged a hand over his head. "You're right. I should have been honest."

"I'm leaving."

"Without your shoes?"

Brianne wagged a finger at him. "Don't talk to me." And then she turned, running to the front door.

"Come on, Brianne," Alex called after her. She wouldn't get far. Not without her shoes. "Hear me out."

She threw the door open and charged outside.

Alex trotted to the doorway. "If you'll let me explain . . ."

Brianne was sprinting across his lawn toward the sidewalk.

"Damn it, Brianne," Alex muttered.

He contemplated chasing her but knew that right now he had to step back and give her her space.

She would be back. She just needed some time.

CHAPTER 15

When, an hour and a half later, Brianne hadn't returned, Alex got worried. He grabbed the car keys and left the house, determined to find her.

After all, she couldn't have gone far. Not in her bare feet.

But what if she was so despondent that she had put herself in harm's way?

The thought had Alex quickening his pace. He rushed into the Navigator and started it without hesitation.

You screwed this up royally, didn't you, Alex?

He drove along every street in the neighborhood and saw no sign of her. That's when his stomach tightened and he truly began to panic.

Had she been easy prey for a stalker on the prowl?

"Damn it, Brianne. Where are you?"

She wouldn't have made her way to Dean Knight's office, would she? Perhaps — if she was desperate to talk to the man.

His search exhausted, Alex drove back to his house. He was going to grab his cell, where he could retrieve Dean's number. If Dean or Ginny hadn't seen her, then he would have to call the police.

Alex turned into his driveway. Before the Navigator had come to a complete stop, he had the door open. He was charging for the house when a glimpse of pink at the side near the hedges caught his eye.

Was that . . . ?

His stomach flinching, Alex started in that direction.

As he got closer to the side of the house, relief washed over him in waves. Yes, he had seen the pink fabric of a shirt.

Brianne's shirt.

He rushed forward. Brianne was sitting with her knees drawn to her chest. Her body had been almost entirely blocked by the brick wall, except for that small bit of her shirt.

"Thank God." Alex dropped down onto his haunches in front of her. "Bree, I've been so worried."

She didn't even acknowledge him, as if she were a mannequin and not a person. But her eyes were puffy from crying, showing that she was very much alive.

Alex wrapped his arms around her, pulling her to her feet. "Come inside."

She said nothing, but at least she didn't fight him.

Alex lifted her and carried her into the house. He brought her up to the bedroom, where he laid her on the bed.

She immediately turned her back to him and dragged the pillow over her face.

"I'm sorry, Bree," Alex said. "God knows, I feel awful for hurting you."

She didn't respond. For several seconds Alex watched her, finally deciding that it was best to let her rest. He made his way to the door. But as he crossed the threshold, he heard Brianne speak.

"Then why did you?"

Alex turned. "Pardon me?"

"You say you feel bad for hurting me. So why did you? Why did you lie knowing what it would do to me?"

Slowly, Alex walked back toward the bed. "Because once I realized that Carter was likely alive, I needed answers. Answers about —"

"And to get your answers, you didn't care how it would hurt me." She spoke in a deadpan voice, as though void of emotion. Alex would have preferred her wrath.

"No, that's not true."

"Isn't it?"

Alex moved forward, aching to reach for her. He wanted to fold her into his arms and hold her until all her pain was gone. But he didn't dare touch her. Because he knew the gesture would ring hollow.

"You've had a rough couple of hours. Get some rest. When you get up, we'll talk."

"When I get up, I'll be leaving."

"Brianne, we are this close to finding Carter." Alex held his forefinger and thumb an inch apart.

"Carter was cheating on me. You said so. Which means the chances of he and I getting back together are slim to none. And even if he'd have me, I would never have him. So there's no reason for me to be here." She paused, giving him a pointed look. "And you'll have to forgive me if I'm not exactly fond of spending more time with you."

Alex closed his eyes. Thought of how to respond. He reopened them, saying, "You said you hate me and . . . and I understand that." His stomach lurched as he said the words. Could she truly hate him, after the way she had connected with him? "Honestly, I wish I could have done this without deceiving you. Maybe I could have, but my gut told me you wouldn't have helped me if

I'd told you the truth."

"It's all about you, right? To hell with anyone else."

"I needed to find Carter." Alex spoke earnestly, imploring her to understand. "And with your link to Tracy — I couldn't remember her name, by the way — I knew you could probably be the one to lead me to her."

"So you didn't even care about my needs at all. You simply used me."

Alex lowered himself onto the bed. Brianne wiped at tears that were falling onto the pillow.

"Bree, I didn't . . ." He stopped himself. But hadn't he? He *had* used her, even if he'd been too single-minded in his focus to see that that was what he was doing.

"I'm going to tell you something, Bree, and I hope it helps you understand my motives. When I saw Carter on TV and realized that he had likely staged his whole disappearance, I also realized that he had to be the one who had set up the robbery at our store while we were on our trip. It all suddenly made sense. How the thieves knew exactly where in the store the safe was hidden. Carter had to be the one who —"

Brianne jerked her body upright. "You put me through this hell because you wanted to get some money back?"

"No," Alex answered softly. "This isn't about the money. I couldn't care less about the money. It was replaced by insurance anyway."

"So what, then?" Brianne's tone was incredulous. "What on earth could be so important that you had such little concern for me that you would hurt me this way?"

"One thing in the safe was irreplaceable," Alex told her. "One thing Carter knew was more important to me than all the money in the world. An antique ring my mother left me on her deathbed." He paused, feeling anger and bitterness and the overwhelming sense of sadness he always did when he thought of the loss. "That ring . . . it had been passed down through the generations and meant the world to my mother. And it means the world to me for sentimental reasons. That's why I knew I had to do what I could to find Carter to get that ring back . . . even if that meant keeping the truth from you."

Brianne lowered her head onto the pillow. "I don't want to talk anymore."

Turbulent feelings rolled through Alex like a freight train. Feelings he wasn't used to.

He wanted to ask her if she understood his motives. Mostly he wanted to ask her to forgive him. But he didn't want to push her, didn't want to make her run.

"All right. I'll be downstairs. Whenever you're ready to talk. If you want."

Brianne closed her eyes. Alex watched the heavy rise and fall of her chest and wondered if she had meant what she'd said.

If she really hated him.

Because if the cost of getting his mother's ring back was Brianne's hate, then maybe this whole mission hadn't been worth it.

Brianne didn't think that anything Alex said would have calmed her ire, but the story about his mother's ring got to her, tugging at her heartstrings.

When she had run from his house, she had wanted to never stop. To run so far that she could escape the pain his words had caused.

But that was impossible. There was no place on earth she could outrun what Alex had told her.

Carter had been cheating on her. He had proposed but had been sleeping with her former friend, Tracy. That knowledge burned her at her very core.

But there was also a part, deep in her soul, where the words were like the final pieces to a puzzle. She had sensed that something had changed between her and Carter.

Sensed it without knowing what it was. And silly her, she'd believed that *she* had been the cause for whatever rift was growing between them.

She would ask him questions, and he always said she was smothering him, trying to create problems where there were none. Fearful of losing him, Brianne had pulled back, but she still had felt that something was . . . off.

Was it ever. Carter had been lying to her for God only knew how long. He had proposed to her, yet he'd been playing her for a fool.

But why? That was the question that had plagued her as she'd wandered barefoot around the neighborhood. When the soles of her feet began to hurt, she returned to Alex's house, but there was no way she was going inside. She wasn't ready to see him. So she'd sat on the grass at the side of the house, thinking about everything and crying.

Alex had asked her if she was truly so devastated to learn of Carter's betrayal three years after the fact. Her initial thought was yes, of course she was that upset. But as the hours had passed and she considered his question, Brianne realized that wasn't exactly true. The truth was, she could probably deal with the news of Carter's betrayal, but what had really hurt her was the way that Alex had used her.

She cared about Alex. As startling as that reality was, it was true. Somewhere along the way she had discovered that she was fiercely attracted to him.

Rather, she had stopped denying the obvious.

It was just that she couldn't understand it. And yet, the feeling was oddly familiar. As if it wasn't a new attraction, but an old one.

Brianne felt a shocking jolt, as if she'd been struck by lightning.

Had she been attracted to Alex before?

Oh, dear God. What am I thinking?

And yet, there was something right about the revelation. On some level, she knew it had the ring of truth.

Perhaps not a fully fledged attraction — they hadn't had the opportunity to explore it before. But there had definitely been a spark of interest the first moment she'd seen him.

That very first moment — seeing him smile at her in the store — something inside of her had melted. And then Carter had suddenly approached her, speaking to her first.

Alex was wrong. She didn't hate him. She was angry, definitely. But the story he'd told her about the stolen ring did strike a chord with her. He'd spoken so fondly of his mother, Brianne could only imagine that it was a crushing blow to have lost an heirloom so important to her.

But he should have told her the truth. Laid it on the line and trusted that she would help him.

Brianne paced the bedroom floor, another thought taking shape in her mind. Was that what all his kisses were about? A way to butter her up so she would be more likely to forgive him *his* betrayal?

Had he led her on emotionally as a way to achieve his end goal?

Brianne stopped pacing and gripped her stomach, the very thought making her feel ill.

Because if Alex could be so callous as to manipulate her on an emotional level, then that would be the worst betrayal of all.

CHAPTER 16

Alex hadn't been sleeping. So when he heard what sounded like a door opening, he immediately eased up on an elbow and paid closer attention. Ever since he'd brought a plate of food to Brianne's door and said good night to her, he had been worried that she would try to take off in the night.

Was that another sound? A moment later, when his door opened, Alex had his answer.

Brianne was standing there in the darkness. Alex quickly glanced at his digital clock. Three-thirteen in the morning. Had she come to tell him that she was leaving?

"Alex?" she called softly. "Are you awake?"

He sat up. "Yeah, I'm awake."

Brianne stepped into the room. It was then that Alex saw she was wearing only a T-shirt.

"Brianne," Alex said, surprised at how breathless he sounded. "What are you doing here?"

She walked slowly toward him, and Alex's breathing became shallow. There was something about her movements, something deliberate.

Something arousing.

She didn't answer his question. Instead, she eased down on the bed beside him, her eyes holding his.

Was he dreaming? Maybe Brianne was a figment of his imagination.

Her hand reached forward. Stroked his cheek.

It certainly felt real.

"Brianne —"

She placed a finger on his lips to silence him. "No. Don't say anything."

And then she leaned her face forward and kissed his cheek.

Alex would have been certain he was dreaming — if his body hadn't totally come alive. He was awake. No doubt about it.

And Brianne was stroking his cheek.

Why? was the question he wanted to ask. She had just learned the truth about Carter. She'd told him she hated him. So why was she here in his room, beside him on his bed, stroking him as if she wanted to seduce him?

Brianne leaned forward. This time she kissed the edge of his mouth. And when she moved her lips to the underside of his jaw, all rational thought fled his mind.

She wanted him. And he wanted her. He wasn't going to question it, even though he couldn't believe it.

He snaked an arm around her waist, pulling her onto the bed with him.

"I've been so blind," Brianne whispered into his ear. "All this time, it should have been you."

Alex had been running a palm over her thigh, but his hand stilled. His entire body went still. "Wh-what did you say?"

"You're the one I should have been with. Not Carter."

Wonder filled him. Was this really true? Perhaps he was dreaming after all. Alex framed her face, staring at her beauty in the moonlit room. She was real in his arms, looking at him with white-hot desire.

He drew her to him and kissed her hungrily.

She kissed him back with abandon, wrapping her arms tightly around his neck. Her mouth was wide, giving him total access to the soft recesses of her mouth.

Brianne shifted, moving her delectable body onto his. Alex groaned in pure pleasure, growing rock hard with the knowledge that this was really happening.

He nibbled her bottom lip. Suckled it. Kissed a hot path to her ear and flicked his tongue over her lobe.

Heat engulfed Brianne. Her entire body was on fire, her need for Alex stronger than anything she had ever felt before.

He kissed her lips again, his tongue tangling with hers, his excited groans making her entire body throb.

Alex broke the kiss and eased back to stare at her. "I feel like I'm dreaming." He was breathless. "I keep wondering if this is really happening."

Brianne felt like she was dreaming as well. As if she had sleepwalked into Alex's bedroom and joined him on his bed.

She honestly wasn't sure how she'd gone from being angry to being in his arms.

She didn't want to think, only feel. Leaning forward, she kissed him again. He growled, a low and hungry sound. He wanted her, just as much as she wanted him.

What was happening between them was real. It had to be. Surely Alex wasn't faking what he felt for her.

He ran his hands down her back, then splayed them over the small of her back, pulling her against the rock hard evidence of his desire for her. His tongue delved into her mouth as far as it could go.

It wasn't enough.

She maneuvered her legs over his body, straddling him. Alex ran his fingers through her hair, still kissing her senseless. The bed sheet was between their bodies, and Brianne desperately wanted to feel his skin against hers.

Tearing his lips from hers, he rasped, "If you don't want this, stop it now."

In response, Brianne gyrated her pelvis against him and kissed the underside of his jaw.

Alex groaned in pleasure, and Brianne felt a surge of power. There was something completely thrilling about knowing that she could seduce a man like Alex.

He was tall, dark and handsome — and she was tired of trying to deny that there was something between them.

And she wanted more than anything to know that he felt something for her.

As she continued to kiss his jawline, creating what she knew was a path of wonderful sensations all the way to his ear, he gripped her butt and squeezed the flesh. When his finger slipped beneath the edge of her panties, a jolt of heat went straight to her center.

Suddenly, she was being eased onto her back, the sheets were being kicked aside and then Alex was on top of her. Every nerve ending in her body was on fire. Her breathing was ragged as he stared down at her. As she saw the obvious lust in his eyes.

But not just lust. There was something else there. Something tender. Surely she wasn't imagining it.

"Make love to me," she whispered.

That was all Alex needed to hear before slipping his hands beneath her nightshirt. He smoothed his palms over her hips, moving upward. His hands heated a path over her rib cage to the underside of her breasts, at which point a slow breath oozed out of her.

"My God, you're so beautiful."

His words flowed over her like warm chocolate, rich and sweet. And the look in his eyes. He regarded her like she was a priceless piece of art.

With deliberate skill, he ran the tip of his finger over the fullness of her breast before gently touching her nipple. Brianne gasped. His touch was light, but it was electric.

He met her eyes while he ran the tip of his finger around her areola. His eyes made her feel just as hot as his finger was making her feel.

He kissed her. A tender yet passionate kiss. Deep and oh, so fulfilling. When he was finished, he tugged Brianne's T-shirt upward until it was out of the way.

Then he lowered his head, taking his time, and Brianne held her breath. When the first flick of his hot tongue hit her nipple, she began to writhe.

She moaned as he suckled her nipple slowly, exquisitely. It was clear to Brianne that he did nothing hurried. He didn't believe in rushing. Gentle flicks, little nibbles — his mouth was driving her wild. As he pleased her with his teeth and tongue, he brought his other hand to her other breast, teasing the nipple into a hardened peak.

Brianne's head moved from side to side. Nothing had ever felt as good as this. Nothing. Something about Alex's touch electrified her body in a way she had never known.

He moved his mouth to the other nipple, pleasing her until she was panting from the unbelievable pleasure. Breathless, she didn't think she could take any more.

And then he began to move his lips down her body, over her belly, dipping his tongue into her belly button as his hands slipped beneath the sides of her panties.

The excitement, the sensations — it was as if Brianne were experiencing this for the first time. It had been so long, she had forgotten how delicious it could be to make love.

But as Alex dragged her panties down her thighs, she knew that wasn't true. She hadn't forgotten. The truth was that Alex's touch made her feel like she was experiencing something brand new.

Alex kissed her inner thigh, and Brianne's body tensed. Again he kissed and nibbled. The man knew how to use his teeth in a gentle yet thrilling way.

He kissed her other thigh. Sucked on her flesh. Brianne's breath came in hurried pants.

Tenderly, he touched her center. Brianne flinched.

"You're beautiful," he whispered. "Incredible."

When Brianne felt the heat of his breath on her most sensitive spot, her eyes fluttered shut. And then she felt the heat of his tongue there, and she thought she would die from the overwhelming pleasure.

Alex pleased her until she was gripping the bed sheets and crying out his name, her body quivering from an earth-shattering orgasm.

Only when he knew she was completely satisfied did Alex ease back. He stretched his body across to the night table. It took

Brianne a moment to realize that he was getting a condom from the drawer.

Brianne stared at him. Stared at this man who had made her feel more incredible than any man ever had.

He must have misconstrued the look in her eyes, because he said, "It's not that I was planning this . . . but I —"

"Shh." Brianne placed a finger on his lips. She didn't care if he had been thinking about this moment ahead of time. She was just glad that he'd been thoughtful enough to think of protection. "All I'm thinking right now is how much I want to be with you." She paused, smiled up at him. "And I'm thinking something else."

"What?" Alex asked, stroking her face.

"I'm thinking . . . wondering . . . what would have happened if you'd talked to me first that day."

"I would have made you mine and never let you go."

Brianne moaned softly, the statement arousing her even more.

Alex leaned over her and kissed her deeply, then he stood and stripped out of his briefs. Brianne watched him, a delicious rush washing over her as she saw him in his full naked glory. As he began to slip the condom on, she pulled the T-shirt over her head.

Alex emitted a raw, sexual growl as his own eyes drank in the sight of her nakedness. Had Brianne ever felt more sexy?

She lay backward and he devoured her mouth as he settled between her thighs, bringing the passion between them to a fever pitch.

He entered her slowly, filling her completely. And Brianne knew that as long as she lived, no one would ever make her feel this amazing.

For the next hour, they made sweet love. It was intense, yet it was tender. They gave and received the pleasure that a man and woman were meant to give to each other.

Every stroke, every touch, every sigh and moan had meaning. Far more than Brianne had ever anticipated.

Finally, their bodies spent, they lay together, wrapped in each other's arms as if that was where they were both meant to be.

Brianne was satisfied beyond measure.

But she was also afraid.

She wasn't sure of all the reasons why she had come into Alex's bed, except that at the time she'd been looking for an escape from her pain. Her emotions were all over the place, and she'd needed the kind of distraction where she wouldn't have to think for a while.

She'd gotten something else.

Proof that she had feelings for Alex.

And that thought scared her to death.

CHAPTER 17

Alex awoke slowly. In the moments before full consciousness, he had the sense of total contentment.

His eyes flew open, the memory of last night hitting him full force. Brianne . . .

His head jerked to his left. She wasn't in the bed with him, and for the briefest of moments Alex wondered if last night had been a dream.

But her scent lingered on his sheets. He could almost still feel her in his arms.

No, it wasn't a dream. Last night had been real.

He threw the covers off of his naked body. Standing, he stretched. He was tired, but it was a good kind of tired.

Because he'd made love to Brianne, and it had been the best experience of his life.

Where was she? In the shower?

Alex slipped into his briefs and made his way to the door. She was up. He could hear her in the hallway.

Smiling, he opened the door and stepped into the hallway, ready to scoop her into his arms and plant a deep kiss on her. But when he saw her, his smile faltered.

Brianne was heading toward the stairs. With her suitcase.

Her eyes widened, indicating she was surprised to see him, and perhaps a little panicked. She quickly looked toward the opening to the stairs, then back at him, then at the stairs again — and Alex could tell she was debating whether or not to make a run for it.

What the heck?

He wasn't about to let her leave. Stepping toward her, he asked, "Brianne, where are you going?"

She opened her mouth but said nothing. Then she sighed. "I think it's best I leave."

Alex looked at her with the same expression he would have had she grown a second head. "What are you talking about?"

"Don't try to talk me out of it."

Alex was flummoxed. "Last night, you were purring in my arms. Now you're trying to slip out without even saying bye?"

"Last night was —"

"Don't say it."

"— a mistake," Brianne finished. She said

the words with difficulty, glancing at the floor as she spoke.

"It sure as hell was not." Alex stepped toward her, and she instinctively took a step backward.

"Alex, please."

"Please what? Please kiss that spot behind your ear that drives you wild? Please give it to you —"

"Stop!" Brianne cried, her heart thundering. Hearing the words she'd uttered in the throes of passion was too much right now. She didn't want to remember a single thing about the spectacular time she'd spent in Alex's bed.

Because she'd woken up with a new clarity. The clarity that she needed to take a step backward. How long had she loved Carter, even after he'd disappeared? Suddenly she was feeling something for Alex? It didn't make sense. Clearly, what she'd believed to be attraction was her mind's way of coping with a totally stressful situation.

"Don't leave, Brianne. Not after what happened between us last night."

His soft plea touched a spot deep inside of her. But she steeled her jaw and said, "Last night was about . . . about needing an outlet for stress."

"So I was just an outlet for you?" Alex

asked, his voice tinged with incredulity.

He was more than that. Too much more. Which was exactly what scared her so much. "Yes."

"You said that it always should have been me."

Oh, God. She *had.* "I . . . I didn't mean it. Words of passion, that's all."

"Wow."

"What do you expect? You'd just told me the truth about Carter, and the fact that you'd lied to me —"

"And then you crawled into my bed and seduced me. Forgive me for thinking we'd turned a corner."

Brianne's face flushed hotly. How could she make him understand? Make him understand that she didn't trust herself and sure as hell wasn't ready to trust what she thought she was feeling for him.

"I'm sorry," Alex said. "Is that what you want me to say? You want me to apologize again?"

"Oh, don't give me that self-righteous tone," Brianne retorted, calling on her anger. She needed to be angry. That was the only way she would remain objective around Alex, because Lord knew, just one of his looks made her knees buckle. "Just because we ended up in bed doesn't change the issue. You lied to me. You had me come down here with you on what I thought was an attempt to find Carter. But all the while, you had another agenda."

"We talked about this last night."

"So it shouldn't bother me?" Alex looked confused, and Brianne knew he had to be. Truly, she couldn't say anything that would explain why — if she was still angry with him — she had ended up in his bed.

"Would you have come here with me had I told you the truth?" Alex asked. "Would you have gotten on a plane and come to Florida with me, knowing what we'd find?"

Brianne thought only for a moment, then said, "No. Never."

"There you go," Alex said. "That's why I did it. Because I needed you to say yes. Bree, we've gone over this."

"Until a couple of months ago, I thought I was still in love with Carter. But I finally decided I could no longer put my life on hold." She lifted her gaze to him. "And when you came to see me, everything I had hoped and prayed for was finally coming true. You thought Carter was alive, and I . . ."

Her voice trailed off. She moved to the banister and gripped it, staring down to the foyer below.

"And you what?" Alex asked gently.

She faced him. "I shouldn't have fallen into bed with you last night. I was confused and needed comfort . . . and you were there."

If she had sliced him with a razor, it would have hurt less. "I don't believe that," Alex said. Maybe he was stubborn or hopelessly pathetic, but he refused to believe her words. He had felt every bit of her passion for him last night, and he knew it was real.

"And it's hard to say no to a woman hell-bent on seduction, isn't it?" she went on. "I can't stay because there's obviously some sort of attraction between us, something I don't understand, and the last thing I want to do is get caught up in emotions based on a lie."

"A lie? Nothing about last night was a lie — at least not for me."

"Don't . . . don't say things you don't mean."

Alex closed the distance between them, curling his hand around the back of her head. "Do you know how many times I wished I'd made it to you first?" he asked quietly. "How many times I regretted that I wasn't fast enough? It wasn't just that I knew Carter was the charmer, that he would woo you the way he had other women. It was that I knew he'd hurt you. But I . . . I never would have hurt you, Bree."

Brianne's heart was pounding so hard, she thought she might go into cardiac arrest. "But you did hurt me."

"The truth hurt you. And I'm sorry for that. But if I'd told you the truth that day I went to your place in Buffalo, would you even have believed me?"

Brianne's mouth opened. She wanted to say yes, that she would have believed him. But she knew suddenly that she wouldn't have. She was angry with him on principle, but Alex was right. If he'd dropped his bombshell about Carter that day, she would have sent him away and maybe cut off all communication with him.

It was what she'd done before.

At the time, she wouldn't have been willing to believe the truth about Carter from a man she'd never had a close relationship with. Now that she'd spent day and night with Alex, learned that he wasn't the cold, unfeeling playboy Carter had made him out to be, she had grown to trust him.

Do you know how many times I wished I'd made it to you first?

Had he really just said those words to her? Her body tingled with a growing sense of excitement.

242

"I don't know what to believe, Alex."

"Believe this." Gently, he framed her face. He stared deeply into her eyes as if trying to convince her without words just how he felt about her. And then he lowered his face to hers.

Brianne thought he would kiss her lips. Instead, he pressed his soft lips to her forehead.

How could such a soft touch elicit such a heated reaction in her body?

"How can I want this?" she asked. The question was rhetorical. "How can I want you when I held on to my love for Carter for so long?"

"Maybe because you knew that one day I would come back into your life."

God, was he right? Had she always known this day would come? And had she been so unable to face the reality of her attraction for Alex that she had always hidden behind anger when dealing with him?

She didn't know what to think. All she knew as Alex circled his arms around her waist and softly kissed her cheek was that there was a part of her that felt like she was finally right where she was supposed to be.

But that niggling doubt returned. The doubt of her feelings. How could she have been in love with Carter and now falling for his best friend?

Brianne started to pull back, but Alex tightened his grip around her. "No," he said softly. "Don't pull away."

She stared up at him, looking into eyes that were heated with the kind of desire for her she didn't ever remember seeing in Carter's eyes.

"I . . . I . . ."

"Do you want me to stop?"

A challenge. The kind he knew he would win, given the way his fingers splayed on her back now. "I don't want to get hurt," she told him honestly. Because he had the power to hurt her far worse than Carter ever had.

"I meant what I said," he told her. "You don't know how many times I wish I'd made it to you first that day in the store. In fact, I've never stopped wishing it."

What was he saying? And why was she loving the way she felt in his arms?

She could dismiss last night's actions as desperate need, but how did she explain that right now she wanted nothing more than to sleep with him again?

"I loved Carter like a brother and would never have fought him for you, even if I thought he would hurt you. But that was then, Bree. He's not a friend anymore."

Brianne tried to digest what he was telling her. That he'd always been attracted to her. But that because of his friendship with Carter, he had never dared to pursue her. But that the stakes had changed and there were a whole new set of rules.

"If you really want me to let you leave, just say the word," he continued. "Say the word, and I will."

Brianne parted her lips, but no sound came. The truth was, she didn't want to protest anything. Instead, she wanted to give in to the wild urge telling her to slip her hands into the edges of Alex's briefs and drag them down his legs.

"You asked why I haven't dated seriously," Alex said softly, lowering his face to hers. "Because I've never felt as strong an attraction to another woman as I did to you the first day I saw you."

His words were a potent aphrodisiac, turning her on, making her wet. If he was lying, then he was one of the most skilled liars on the planet.

Right now, she didn't care. The only thing she wanted was to get naked and make love to him again.

She placed her palms on his muscular chest. Beneath her fingertips, she could feel the pulsing beat of his heart.

She stroked one of his flat nipples and was rewarded with a low groan. Leaning forward, she planted her lips on his smooth, hard chest. She let her lips linger there a moment before flicking the tip of her tongue over his skin. He tasted salty, a mix of his own perspiration and the sweat both their bodies had created together while making love.

"Come here," he growled. Lifting her chin upward, he brought his mouth down on hers. Hard.

Lord, the sensations that filled her were oh, so wonderful. How was it that she had been betrothed to Carter, and yet she had never felt this electric thrill whenever he kissed her, much less touched her.

Alex slipped his hands beneath Brianne's buttocks and urged her upward. The next thing she knew, she was wrapping her legs around his waist and he was carrying her to the nearby bedroom.

He lowered her on the bed, his mouth locked with hers. He kissed her while he slipped his hands beneath her shirt, his touch sending shivers of delight all over her skin. He kissed her as his fingers found her nipples. Kissed her as he tweaked them into hardened peaks.

"I can't get enough of you," he rasped and

moved his mouth to her neck, where he suckled her flesh until she was whimpering.

"I want you naked," he told her.

Brianne had never been particularly comfortable with her body and always preferred making love in the dark with Carter. But with the sunlight spilling into the room, Brianne sat up and pulled off her shirt. Then she unsnapped her bra. All while Alex's eyes were glued to her body.

She didn't feel self-conscious. She felt beautiful and desirable.

As she shimmied her jeans over her hips, Alex took his briefs off. Brianne stared at his body without shame as he put a condom on. He was large and hard and the definition of sexy.

And he was about to be hers once more.

The moment she was fully naked, Alex moved to her, reaching for both of her breasts at the same time. He kneaded them gently, squeezed them together, flicked his thumbs over her sensitive peaks. Brianne gripped his shoulders for support, knowing that if he continued to please her this way she would be weak with desire and unable to support her own weight.

Alex lowered his head to her right breast and grazed her nipple with his teeth. She threw her head back and cried out from the sweet sensation.

Alex pleasured both breasts with his fingers and his tongue, until Brianne was digging her fingers into his flesh and on the edge of falling into a pit of endless bliss. Then Alex kissed her, got on the bed on his back and pulled her on top of him. He guided their bodies together, and Brianne whimpered, knowing she was close. He held her hips as he thrust upward, filling her body and also her soul.

"Open your eyes," Alex said.

Brianne did.

"You're beautiful, baby." He stroked her nipples, heightening her pleasure. "So beautiful."

His words were her undoing. Brianne tumbled into the abyss, lost in a whirlwind of delicious sensations.

As her entire body savored the wonderful climax, she became aware of one undeniable fact.

She had fallen for Alex.

She was in love with him.

CHAPTER 18

Brianne and Alex spent the rest of the morning in bed, making love until they both had no more energy. They napped in each other's arms and this time woke up together.

Brianne wasn't running anymore.

As much as she wanted nothing more than to spend the rest of the day making love with this incredible man, she knew that it was time to get on with the business they had to deal with. She wanted to move on past Carter once and for all, and that meant finding him, confronting him and getting the closure she deserved.

"When I knew Tracy, she worked for Marriott," Brianne told Alex as she trailed her fingers over his chest. She was lying in the crook of his arm, a place she could comfortably stay forever. "Her full name is Tracy Salmon."

"Like the fish?" Alex asked.

"And just as slimy," Brianne couldn't help saying.

"Think of the bright side," Alex said, and Brianne made a face as she looked at him. "If not for Tracy, you and Carter might still be together. And we most certainly would not be here like this right now."

Brianne grinned from ear to ear. "And you are definitely the hottest silver lining I've ever known."

Alex ran his fingers through her short hair, and Brianne curled her face into his palm. Suddenly she became serious. "Why do you think he did it? I mean, it can't be just because he wanted to be with Tracy. All he had to do was dump me."

"I've been thinking about that ever since I saw him on television. There was the robbery, but we only had about a hundred grand in the safe. Carter was worth more than that. There was also my mother's ring, but again, it wasn't worth seven figures or anything. Ultimately I figured it must have been a scam to capitalize on a major insurance policy."

"In seven years? There was no body. Doesn't it take at least seven years for a person to be declared dead when they're missing?"

"Normally. But I did some investigating,

and it turns out that there are times when the court will declare a person dead based on imminent peril — if the family petitions the court for a death certificate."

Brianne considered something. "Do you think Tracy was the beneficiary of Alex's life insurance policy?"

"I wouldn't doubt it. Especially if he's down here with her."

Brianne sat up, and again she was struck by just how comfortable she was being naked in front of Alex. "What do you say? Should we start calling the Marriott hotels in Daytona and seeing if we can track Tracy down?"

"There's no time like the present."

After checking the Marriott hotels in the Daytona area with no luck, Brianne and Alex extended their search to Orlando, which was only an hour away. And they struck pay dirt, finding that a Tracy Holden worked as a manager at a hotel in North Orlando.

It was the only Tracy in a managerial position, and since it made sense that she and Carter had likely changed names to create new identities, they assumed that Tracy Holden was the Tracy they were seeking.

She was due to finish work at 6:00 p.m.,

and Alex and Brianne hit the road with enough time to make it to the hotel before she left.

At five-thirty, after killing time at a local bookstore, they drove into the hotel's parking lot. Brianne's stomach danced with nerves.

She stared toward the front entrance as Alex parked the Navigator in an available spot. "So," she said, the word heavy. "Here we are. What's your plan? To go inside and talk to Tracy? See if she'll tell us the truth about Carter?"

"Naw," Alex answered. "I think the better idea is to wait for her. When she comes out, we follow her. It'll be the end of her workday. I'm sure she'll be heading home. So we follow her and find out where she lives."

Brianne nodded. "I guess that makes sense."

"Brianne, if you're not sure you can do this, I can take you back to the bookstore and pick you up later."

"No way," Brianne said. "I am *so* ready to confront Carter. And Tracy as well."

Alex reached across the front seat and covered her hand with his.

She drew in a heavy breath. He knew she was nervous. He was nervous, too. He had no clue how things would play out when he saw Carter again.

Once, he had loved Carter like a brother. He should be elated to know that his old friend was alive. Yet what he felt was a deep sense of betrayal and anger.

"I hope you get your mother's ring back," Brianne said softly. "If Carter was motivated by greed, he could have pawned it."

"I know." Alex gritted his teeth and gazed forward. "I'm not sure what I'll do if that's the case."

"You really loved your mother."

Alex met Brianne's gaze. "She was the most important woman in my life. Every time I told her that, she would joke that a hot young woman would come along who would snag that title. I always told her no. That she'd always be number one."

A soft smile touched Alex's lips as he talked about his mother, but there was also pain in his expression. Brianne's heart ached for him. She had always heard the saying that a woman should go for a man who loved and respected his mother, because he would love and respect her. Carter had barely talked about his mother. The two obviously weren't close. Ultimately, he had disrespected Brianne. On the other hand, Alex clearly adored his mother, and Brianne could tell that he believed in treating women with kindness and respect.

Yes, he had lied to her, but no one was perfect. And she understood his motive, given that it was driven by the love for the mother he'd lost too soon.

"I still remember the day we learned she only had a few months to live. For so long, I'd held out hope. My dad, too. We both believed that our love could save her." Alex sighed softly. "The doctors tried everything, but in the end, nothing worked to save her. It's hell to see someone you love go through something like that. To know you're going to lose them, and there's not a damn thing you can do about it."

"I'm so sorry," Brianne said. Her eyes misted with tears. "I can't imagine losing someone you love that way."

"She was ready. She'd made peace with her illness and with God. But I wasn't ready. Not even close. I wanted her to keep fighting, to try alternative treatments. And then I realized that I was being selfish. She was tired of it all. She knew there was no hope, and she was ready to let go."

Brianne squeezed Alex's hand.

"One of the last things she did was give me that ring and tell me to make sure I gave it to the woman I wanted to spend the rest of my life with. I vowed that I would."

"And Carter knew this?"

"Yeah," Alex said softly. "He knew."

"Oh, Alex."

"I've never been the kind of guy who was into dating woman after woman, just for the sake of having a warm body in my bed. More than anything I just want to find that special person my mother always wanted me to find, and spend my life having the kind of relationship my parents had."

Want to find . . . As if he hadn't found it already. Brianne's stomach twisted.

"Bree, is that her?"

Brianne jerked her head around, following Alex's line of sight. And there was Tracy, the tall, thin, pretty woman who had once been her best friend. Her hair had blond highlights and was pulled back in a ponytail.

"Yes," Brianne said, nerves making her skin tingle. "That's her."

She walked to a sleek, black BMW, and if Brianne had had any reservations about Tracy's identity, they were gone now. The car was exactly the kind that Carter would drive.

Tracy got into the vehicle, and Alex started the Navigator. "Time to roll."

CHAPTER 19

Alex kept a good distance behind Tracy as he followed her. There were a couple of times Brianne worried that he'd lose her, but he never did.

Tracy drove into an upscale neighborhood. Not the kind of high-end exclusive neighborhood where Alex's house was, but definitely an area where upper-middle-class people lived. There were lots of Audis, Mercedes and BMWs in the various driveways.

Now that they were in a residential area, Alex slowed down, but he never lost sight of Tracy's car. When he saw her indicate and turn left into a driveway, he pulled up to the curb a good hundred feet back.

"Why are we stopping here?" Brianne asked.

"Just waiting a moment. I don't want her to see us. Once she goes inside, I'll pull into the driveway."

Tracy exited the vehicle and trotted toward her front door. The moment she was inside, Alex drove forward. He was unbuttoning his seatbelt as he turned into the driveway, and Brianne did the same. She could see the determined set of Alex's jaw and couldn't help feeling anxious about what was to come.

They were about to see Carter.

Provided he was home.

And provided she and Alex weren't way off base.

Tracy Salmon Holden. No, they weren't way off base. They were right on the money.

"Ready?" Alex asked.

Brianne nodded. Then she opened her door and hopped out of the Navigator.

Alex took the lead, rushing to the door. Brianne expected him to knock, but instead he turned the knob. Lo and behold, the door opened.

Tracy, who was still standing in the front foyer, whirled around and screamed. Her eyes took in Alex. Then they landed on Brianne, growing wide with recognition.

Beyond Tracy, Carter rushed out of a bedroom, his own eyes wide with worry. But the moment he saw Alex and Brianne, he stopped dead in his tracks.

Alex placed his hands on his hips, enjoying the look of stunned horror on Carter's face. "Surprise, surprise."

Tracy's eyes flitted between Alex and Brianne, as if she expected one of them to pull out a gun. "Carter . . ."

"What's the matter, Tracy?" Brianne said. "Not happy to see me?"

"Come here, babe," Carter called. Tracy rushed toward him, and he wrapped an arm around her. As she clung to his shirt, Alex's heart nearly imploded.

His mother's ring was on Tracy's finger.

"Go sit down," Carter told Tracy. She was already whimpering, clearly terrified. "Sit down," Carter reiterated firmly.

Tracy scurried to the living room, but she didn't sit.

Carter walked toward Alex, the look on his face smug. "So you found me," he said. "It was that bit on ESPN." He shook his head, a sardonic chuckle escaping his throat. "What are the odds you'd have seen that?"

"You were bound to be discovered one day," Alex told him.

Carter looked from Alex to Brianne. "And you're here, too." He shrugged. "Should I be flattered? Have you been holding out hope of finding me alive after three years?"

His smug tone showed he didn't care one lick how he'd hurt Brianne, which enraged Alex. Closing the distance between him and

Carter, he did something that was long over-due.

He drew his hand back and punched him square in the mouth, sending his former friend flying backward against the wall.

Carter rose slowly, bringing a hand to his mouth. Drawing back his hand, he eyed the blood on his fingers. Then he laughed, as if this were all a game. "I bet that felt good, didn't it, Alex?"

"You're damn right it did."

Brianne walked slowly toward Carter. The jerk had the nerve to act smug, even at a time like this. "You're right," she said to him. "I did hold out hope that you were still alive."

Carter smiled. "I knew you would."

"You are the biggest jerk I've ever had the misfortune of knowing." And then she slapped him. Hard.

Instead of looking smug, Carter actually looked surprised.

"Damn you for all you put me through, you selfish, evil cheater!"

Alex put a hand on Brianne's shoulder and gently guided her away from Carter. "It's okay, Brianne. I'll handle this."

Brianne saw when Carter's gaze fell on Alex's hand on her shoulder. She also saw the flash of curiosity.

"Handle?" Carter asked, his eyebrow shooting up. "You came here to handle me? What, beat the crap out of me?"

"I came here to get my mother's ring back. The one your wife is wearing."

Brianne saw Tracy look at the ring on her hand, then at Alex. Finally, she sank onto the sofa.

"Are you sure you came all the way here for a ring?" Carter asked. His eyes volleyed between Alex and Brianne. "Or did you come here to gloat?"

"Gloat?" Alex asked.

Carter nodded toward Brianne. "Looks like you got my girl. And you wanted me to know it."

Alex didn't dignify the question with an answer. "Why did you do it, Carter? Why did you fake your death? For the money?"

"I did what I had to do," he said, nonchalant. "I'm sorry it hurt you, buddy. And you, too, Brianne. But hey. Life goes on. It obviously did for you two."

Alex grabbed Carter by the collar, barely keeping his anger under control. "You piece of dirt. You have no clue what I went through. What Brianne went through. Because of your deception!"

"But you got Brianne, didn't you?"

Alex slammed Carter against the wall. Tracy screamed.

"Fifteen years, man. Fifteen years we were friends. And you could hurt me the way you did? Why? So you could empty our safe of a hundred grand? So you could steal my mother's ring? So you could have a laugh?"

Carter jerked out of Alex's grip. "I already said that I did what I had to do. I don't expect you to understand."

"Because you haven't given us any answers," Brianne snapped.

"I was in debt," Carter said through gritted teeth. "Okay?"

"In debt?" Alex asked. "That doesn't make sense. You were loaded."

"I lost a ton of cash," Carter said. "Gambling. I did some betting with some bookies. At first, it made me money. Next thing I knew, I was losing it all in a flash. I made a lot of enemies. People who wanted to kill me." Carter looked at Brianne. "But I never planned to disappear. I figured I'd take off, head to Brazil or something. Until that day on the mountain when Alex gave me the idea."

"What?" Alex cried.

"Did he tell you what happened that day three years ago?" Carter asked Brianne. He paused a moment, then looked at Alex again. "Did you tell her, Alex? Tell her what happened on the mountain?"

Brianne threw her gaze to Alex, who was steadfastly looking at Carter.

"There is no way in hell I suggested you fake your death."

"Maybe not, but because of you, I got the idea."

Alex looked at Brianne. She was staring at him, the confusion evident on her face.

"Ah, he didn't tell you that we argued," Carter said, and began to smile. "Not only did we argue, he left me on the mountain to die."

Alex grabbed Carter by the collar again. "You low-down, dirty —"

"Go ahead, Alex. Hit me again like you did that day."

"You *hit* him?" Brianne asked, jerking her gaze from Carter to Alex.

Alex said nothing, just glared at Carter.

"Now that I think about it, maybe you were hoping I'd die out there. Because then you could return home and have Brianne all to yourself. Your plan worked like a charm."

"That's a lie!" Alex snapped. He shoved Carter toward the wall, then released him.

Brianne looked at both men in confusion. She didn't understand what they were talking about.

A smirk came over Carter's face, followed by a look that almost resembled anger. Perhaps a smidgen of jealousy. "He slept with you to get back at me, Brianne — after leaving me to die."

"Did you really hit Carter on the mountain?" she asked Alex.

"Yeah, I hit him," Alex admitted. "You should have heard how he was talking about you. Gloating about how you'd make the perfect wife, but that he wasn't giving up his girlfriend."

"So you hit him and you left him on the mountain."

"That's when I knew I could disappear," Carter said. "He'd left me. The snow was coming down. It was the perfect time." Carter paused. "I knew that one day he'd make a play for you."

Alex shot a look at Brianne, saw the disillusionment in her eyes. "Don't listen to him, Brianne. Carter is a skilled liar. For him to get off that mountain undetected, he obviously had a plan in place. He's had three years to spin his lie to make me the villain. In fact . . ." His voice trailed off as reality struck him. "You used *me.* You goaded me into hitting you. You needed us to fight so that we would separate. Then you met with

263

whoever helped you get off the mountain, leaving me to feel a world of guilt."

Alex *knew* that was truth. Felt it in his soul. But the look on Brianne's face said she didn't know what to believe.

"Nice try, Alex. But Brianne's smarter than you give her credit for. Aren't you, Brianne?"

"I am," Brianne agreed, her gaze on Alex.

Alex felt a stab of pain. "Brianne —"

Her gaze moved swiftly to Carter. "Smarter than *you* give me credit for. Obviously you had your plans to disappear. Your store was robbed while you and Alex were on that mountain. That was planned ahead of time. So spare me any more of your lies." She paused. "And if Alex hit you, it was because you deserved it. It's clear he was defending my honor."

Relief washed over Alex. Brianne saw the truth. Thank God. "Yes, Brianne. That's exactly right. I was defending your honor."

"But I'm not sure Carter isn't partially right," she went on.

"What?" Alex asked, stunned.

"I'm not sure I can trust . . . trust what's happened between us. Trust that what we experienced wasn't about . . . revenge."

"That's not true," Alex protested.

"It was all about revenge," Carter said,

egging her on.

"I have to think." Brianne turned and sprang for the door.

Alex started after her and caught hold of her upper arm before she could step outside. "Don't believe Carter. Nothing that happened between us was about revenge."

Brianne's eyes misted with tears. "Are you sure about that?"

"Yes!"

"Well I'm not."

Suddenly Carter was there, standing beside Alex. "Brianne," he began softly. "I'm sorry about . . . everything. I didn't mean to hurt you. I just . . ."

Brianne violently jerked her arm from Alex's grasp and ran outside.

"I may not have Brianne, but it looks like you don't have her either," Carter said smugly.

Alex whirled around to face Carter and saw the self-satisfied expression on his face. And he knew that Carter was goading him.

"I wanted to find you, see for myself if you were really alive. Now that I know you are, I feel sorry for you. Because you're pathetic. You have to live with your conscience. You hurt me, you hurt Brianne, your family. You have to live with that."

"I had debts, Alex. A loan shark after me.

I — I had to do what I did. It was the only way."

In his voice, Alex heard the first inkling of remorse.

"There was another way," Alex countered.

"It wasn't my plan to hurt you."

The sound of a car engine roaring to life made Alex spin around. Brianne was behind the wheel of the Navigator.

Alex looked at his jeans' pocket, where he'd stuck the car key. It was gone.

He charged outside. "Brianne!" Alex yelled. "Brianne, stop!"

She backed out of the driveway like a bat out of hell.

Alex turned back into the house. Carter was suddenly not there. He stalked toward Tracy, saying, "Give me the car key. I've got to get to Brianne."

That's when Carter emerged from a bedroom — with a gun. Directed at Alex. "I don't think so, man."

"Carter, what are you doing?"

"Sorry, man. But I can't let you leave."

CHAPTER 20

It was all about payback.

That was all Brianne could think as she drove erratically through the residential neighborhood.

Alex had used her — not just to find Carter, but to get back at the friend who had hurt him.

The tears fell. They wouldn't stop.

Brianne kept hearing Carter's words, seeing the smug look on his face when he'd said with confidence that he'd known Alex would pursue her. She had been dumb enough to believe that Carter loved her. Had she also been dumb enough to believe that Alex's sweet words had been about a genuine connection, when in fact all she was to him was a pawn in his game to get back at Carter?

Brianne didn't want to believe it — how could she? — but she also knew that what she wanted and reality didn't always equate to the same thing.

She had wanted to believe that Carter loved her, that he had died loving her and looking forward to a life with her. But the truth was, Carter hadn't loved her at all. All the while he'd been seeing Tracy, too, carrying on two different lives.

The knowledge hurt. But strangely, she felt more pain at the thought that what she and Alex had shared had been born of his desire to get back at Carter.

The way he'd made love to her, had held her, had brought her the greatest sexual satisfaction she had ever experienced . . . could it all have been a lie?

It didn't feel like a lie, but clearly she couldn't trust her judgment. She had been a bad judge of character where Carter had been concerned. How could she trust what she felt in her heart about Alex?

Regardless of what she had come to feel for Alex — and perhaps what he had come to feel for her — maybe it was simply best to put both him and Carter behind her. Could she ever have a future with Alex without reliving Carter's deception over and over again in her mind?

After driving around for ten minutes, thinking everything through and examining her feelings, Brianne had a moment of clarity. It was the fight Alex had had with Carter on the mountain that solidified it.

Alex loved her. He had proven that long before she ever knew he cared for her — by defending her honor on the mountain with Carter. Their passion, their love, was real. That was something she knew in her heart with far more certainty than she had ever known anything.

So how could she let him go? Alex may not have been totally truthful with her, but it wasn't because he'd wanted to hurt her. It was because he was also defending his mother's honor in his quest to get her ring back.

If Brianne couldn't understand and accept that, then Alex was the one who should doubt *her* feelings for him.

And she loved him. She had no doubts about that. As she'd told him, he was her silver lining in the dark cloud of pain she had experienced with Carter.

Brianne made a quick U-turn, hoping to retrace the path she'd traveled. She was going back to Carter's house for the man she loved.

And for one other reason.

Tracy.

She hadn't given her former friend a piece of her mind. Brianne might be over Carter

— and as far as she was concerned, he and Tracy deserved each other — but Tracy also deserved a good verbal lashing before Brianne moved on.

She navigated the streets, feeling relief when she realized that she was indeed going the right way.

Minutes later, she pulled into the driveway behind Tracy's car.

It was time that Brianne said her piece. Get the closure she needed.

And then leave with the man she knew she wanted to spend the rest of her life with.

Brianne raised her hand to knock on the door, but before she could, it opened.

Carter faced her. And then he smiled.

"Brianne, you're back. Your boyfriend will be pleased."

Brianne glared at him. "You're not serious. You're not seriously *jealous*."

"It wasn't like I didn't care about you." Carter's eyes traveled over her body. "I've got to say, you look great."

Brianne felt ill under Carter's gaze. She pushed past him and walked into the house. "I have nothing more to say to you. But I do have a few words for Tracy."

As Brianne breezed into the house, she noticed Alex sitting on the sofa.

And Tracy holding a gun.

A wave of fear washed over her.

"Join the party," Carter said, and she heard him lock the door.

Oh, God, no.

"Go on," Carter said. "Take a seat beside your boyfriend. Do it, or Tracy will shoot him."

Brianne's chest began to hurt. She didn't want to step into the living room. But if she didn't, Tracy would kill Alex.

Alex looked at her. Regret swelled inside of her. God, if she hadn't lost track of the truth, if she hadn't fled the house with the need to think, this likely wouldn't have happened.

"Go!" Carter yelled. He grabbed hold of her and dragged her into the living room, where he pushed her onto the sofa beside Alex.

In Alex's eyes, Brianne saw the regret that she felt.

And then she got angry. How dare Carter and Tracy deceive her and now want to kill her and Alex to keep covering up their dirty deception?

"So this is how it ends?" Brianne said defiantly. "It wasn't bad enough that you stole my man, Tracy. Now you're going to put a bullet in me?"

Tracy didn't speak. She looked terrified. Which made Brianne wonder if she would be able to pull the trigger . . .

"Fine, you're going to kill me," Brianne went on. "Answer one thing for me. When did you two hook up? When did you start sleeping with my boyfriend?"

"It's not like you think," Tracy said, her voice low.

"No?" Brianne challenged. "Then tell me how it is. Because there was a time I considered you my best friend. Now you want to kill me?" Brianne hoped that by continuing to stress the reality of what Tracy was about to do, Tracy would see that she *couldn't* commit murder. "Will you look me in the eye and pull the trigger? Is that who you've become?"

"Just be quiet," Tracy said meekly, her eyes flitting in Carter's direction. "Be quiet and everything will be fine."

Carter sat on the chair opposite where Alex and Brianne were seated. He reached into the breast pocket of his shirt and withdrew a cigarette. "By now, you should realize that we'll do whatever's necessary."

"I spent three years of hell grieving you," Brianne said, turning her attention to Carter. "Three years believing that you loved me and wanted a life with me. And yet here

272

you are in Florida, with Tracy. When did it start? When did you start sleeping with my —" Brianne stopped abruptly. Suddenly, she knew. She knew exactly when it had happened.

"That night," she said, standing. "When we'd all gone to dinner. And Tracy called to say she had a flat tire, and then you went back to help her after you dropped me home . . ."

"It wasn't planned," Carter said.

"She was my best friend!"

"We just . . . we clicked."

"Then why didn't you break up with me? Why did you *propose* to me?"

"We didn't want to hurt you."

"Right. You spared me so much pain."

Carter didn't say anything. Just sat silent on his expensive armchair.

But what could he really say? The very reason Tracy and Brianne had fallen out of favor was because Tracy had always been consumed with material things. She probably wouldn't care if Carter had robbed or killed to earn cash, as long as she could drive a luxury car and wear the latest designer clothes.

"Carter." Alex raised his hands slowly. "Give me back my mother's ring, and we'll leave. We'll forget we ever saw you."

"You think I'm stupid?" There was an eerie quality to Carter's voice. "I let you leave, and you go straight to the cops."

"We won't," Alex stressed.

"I'm alive," Carter said. "And yet Tracy collected insurance money two years after my death, after petitioning the court to declare her husband dead."

"Her — her husband?" Brianne asked. The words shouldn't have shocked her, but they did.

"Yes, Brianne," Carter said testily. "We got married. Secretly, before my trip to the Rockies. I needed her not only to be the beneficiary of my life insurance policy, but my wife so she could have authority over my estate."

"And once she settled your life insurance policy and estate, you were both able to change your identities," Alex hypothesized.

"You're the only people standing in our way," Carter said, his voice cold. "And even if Brianne is ready to wash her hands of me, I know you're not, Alex. You'll turn me in for fraud. And I'm sorry, but I can't go to jail."

Brianne stared at Carter, seeing a man she didn't know. But had she ever truly known him?

"You'll never get away with this," Brianne

said. "My sister knows I came down here to find you. If I end up dead, she'll leave no stone unturned until you're in a jail cell."

"I disappeared once. I can do it again."

Brianne faced Tracy. "Are you really going to kill me?"

Tracy didn't reply.

"You kill me, and you have to go on the run somewhere, always looking over your shoulder. Is he worth it?"

Tracy's bottom lip trembled, and Brianne knew she was getting through to her. But she also knew that Carter controlled Tracy ruthlessly. For him to be sitting so calmly smoking a cigarette while *she* held the gun made it clear he believed she would do whatever he wanted her to.

"Do you really want to go to jail for murder, Tracy? Because that's what will —"

"Shut up!" Tracy yelled. She looked like she was on the verge of an emotional breakdown.

No, Tracy didn't want to do this. She was simply following Carter's orders. But would she go as far as to pull the trigger, or would she do the right thing?

Brianne tried a softer approach. "Tracy, you don't want to do this."

One tear made its way down her cheek. "It wasn't supposed to be like this. And

I . . . I never meant to hurt you. But Carter — he made me promises —"

"Shut up, Tracy," Carter said, his tone warning.

"This wasn't the life I expected, always looking over our shoulders," she went on.

"It's not too late to change that." This from Alex.

"Yo, Alex — shut up!"

"You know, Carter, if you want to kill me, you're gonna have to man up and kill me." Alex stood, and Tracy took a step backward. "You take the gun and you shoot me. Me — the guy who was your best friend since eighth grade."

"You'll go down with him either way, Tracy," Brianne said, hoping that Tracy wouldn't hand the gun to Carter but do the right thing and call the police. "You'll go down for a man who doesn't know how to love anyone but himself."

"I love her," Carter said, lurching to his feet. "I always have."

The words shouldn't have hurt Brianne, but they did. Because it was clear now that Carter had never loved *her*. Oh, he may have liked her, but his heart had obviously been with Tracy.

A woman he could control.

"I'm sure your love will be a bright comfort to Tracy when she's staring at the walls of her jail cell," Brianne said.

Tracy's eyes grew wide with horror. It was clear the idea of going to jail was scaring her to death.

Carter stalked toward Brianne. "Enough of your mouth, Brianne. Shut up already."

"When I got here, you told me you never wanted to hurt me," Brianne said simply.

"That's the truth," Carter said.

"And yet you want to kill me now." Her eyes misted, but she didn't turn her head. She continued to hold his gaze. She wanted him to see her pain. To see what it looked like to hurt someone who had given you their total trust and love.

And whatever happened, happened. This was the last time she wanted to get emotional over Carter. Clearly, he didn't deserve any of her tears.

After several beats, she turned to Alex. "But every cloud has its silver lining. Your deception brought me and Alex together. And if all we have is a few minutes left . . . Alex, I want you to know that you're the best thing that ever happened to me. If we die right now, I don't regret coming down here with you. Because I'd rather die having experienced true love for five minutes than spend eighty years never finding it."

All the air left Alex's lungs in a rush. When Brianne had returned, he'd been hopeful that it meant she no longer had any doubts about his feelings for her. But he'd been very aware that she simply might have returned out of obligation — so that she didn't leave him stranded in Orlando. He hadn't been able to gauge the expression on her face, and the danger of the situation had taken precedence over whatever she was feeling. They had shared a couple looks, but he hadn't known what was in her heart.

Now he knew. And despite the very real danger they were facing, happiness filled him like the warm glow of a fire.

"I feel the same way," he told her, and saw her eyes mist with tears. "No matter what happens, this short time with you has been worth it."

"I'm sorry that I doubted you for even one second," Brianne said, her voice cracking. "Doubted us."

"How very touching," Carter scoffed.

Alex once again faced his former friend. "It's not too late to rethink this." He spoke gently, trying to get through to the man he believed had once loved him as a brother. "You committed fraud, but you won't get anywhere near the jail time for that as you'll get for killing us."

Carter seemed to consider the words. Looking conflicted, he began to pace the floor. But after several seconds, he stopped and faced Tracy. "Shoot them," he ordered.

Alex looked at Tracy, whose hands seemed to be trembling. Could he take the chance right now, jump her? Or would the gun go off as he fought to get it from her? He would take the chance of himself getting hurt, but no way did he want to put Brianne at risk.

He decided to stay put and eye her carefully. He would bet his last dollar that she wouldn't pull the trigger. She wasn't a killer.

"Do it," Carter said. "We talked about this, and you told me you could do this if it came down to it. Well, it's them or it's us. I'm the one who took all the risk, setting up a life where we'd be set forever. It's time you get your hands dirty."

So that's what Carter's plan was, Alex thought. To let Tracy do his dirty work. Who knew — maybe he would try to blame Tracy for the devious murder plot if they were ever caught.

The bastard.

"You can't do it," Alex said to Carter, and he couldn't help a self-satisfied chuckle. "You can't look at me and kill me."

Carter didn't meet Alex's gaze. He looked at Tracy and ordered, "Do it already."

Tracy raised the gun higher, and Alex braced himself to make a move. But then she did something that startled Alex. Still holding the gun high, she worked the ring off of her finger and tossed it to Alex. Then, slowly, she turned the gun away from him.

And leveled it at Carter.

"Tracy," Carter began slowly, surprise registering on his face. "What are you doing?"

"I can't live like this anymore," she said, beginning to softly cry. "I'm not going to jail, Carter."

"Babe," he said. "Give me the gun."

"Don't give it to him," Alex said. "You're doing the right thing."

"Give me the gun," Carter repeated and took a tentative step toward her.

"Stop!" she yelled. "Don't come any closer."

"You — you're not going to *shoot* me?" Carter couldn't have sounded more surprised.

She looked toward Alex. "Alex, Brianne. Go on. Get out of here."

"Damn it, Tracy. What the hell are you doing?"

"Shut up!" she yelled at Carter. "And you'd better stay where you are, or I *will* shoot you."

280

Carter couldn't have looked more flummoxed. "For God's sake, Tracy —"

"You think I don't know about Melanie?" she said suddenly, surprising them all. "That you've been sleeping with her?"

Carter's mouth fell open, but he didn't say a word. Not for several seconds. Then, lamely, he said, "She was just a fling."

Tracy began to cry harder. "After everything, Carter — all that I sacrificed . . . how could you?"

"You're the one I love," Carter explained. "Look at everything I did so we could be together."

Alex took a tentative step toward Tracy, knowing that this was the time to gain control. He trusted that Tracy wouldn't shoot him, but he didn't trust Carter not to take the gun from her.

But Carter saw Alex move and lunged at him, growling as he did. Alex wasn't fast enough to jump out of the way, and Carter's shoulder plowed into his solar plexus, knocking him over a nearby ottoman.

Brianne screamed. Maybe both she and Tracy did.

Carter got off a few good punches as Alex tried to gain his bearings. But then Alex threw up his elbow, landing it in Carter's neck.

That knocked Carter off his game, and Alex jumped to his feet, positioning his hands in a boxer's stance, prepared to beat Carter to a pulp if he had to.

That's when the shot went off.

Followed by Brianne's scream.

Alex threw a panicked glance at Brianne, but a quick, frantic once-over told him that she was okay. Then he looked at Tracy, who had tears streaming down her face. Her eyes were fixated on Carter.

Alex then looked directly in front of him. He saw the spot of blood on Carter's side. Carter, looking dazed, brought his hand to his left side and touched the wound. Pulling his hand back, he saw the dark red that covered his fingers, and his expression grew even more confused.

Everyone was absolutely still. No sound permeated the house.

And then Carter fell.

Another scream, followed by a gut-wrenching sob. The gun fell from Tracy's fingers as she dropped to the floor in a weeping heap.

Alex rushed toward her, snatching up the gun from the floor to make sure she wouldn't be able to fire again if she had a change of heart. Either to hurt them or herself.

And then he hurried to Carter, who lay on the floor, blood seeping from his side.

And as much as he hated Carter for what he'd done, he realized that he didn't want it to end this way. He didn't want Carter to die on the floor like this.

He couldn't help but feel a bit of empathy for the man who had once been his best friend.

But he also wanted him to face justice.

"Brianne, call 911!" Alex shouted. He stared down at the man who had betrayed him. He still wore a dazed expression, like he was in shock.

Quickly, Alex lifted Carter's shirt. He examined the wound, then pressed his own hands on Carter's side to help stop the bleeding.

"Hang in there, Carter," Alex said to him. "Because no way am I letting you get off this easy."

CHAPTER 21

Carter didn't die.

But right about now, Brianne was betting that he was wishing that he had.

The list of charges were extensive and included kidnapping on top of the fraud charges. She wasn't sure what would happen to Tracy, who had been inconsolable in the aftermath of the shooting. A detective had told her that if Tracy cooperated, she likely wouldn't face any charges. After all, she had shot Carter when he'd attacked Alex.

But whatever happened to Tracy and to Carter was not Brianne's problem. Her concern was Alex.

They'd both been brought to the police station to be questioned, and Brianne now sat in the waiting room. She wanted desperately to have a moment to talk to him. Ever since the shooting, there had been a flurry of activity, and she wanted him to know that she meant what she'd said.

After another fifteen minutes passed with no Alex, Brianne stood and began to pace in the waiting room. Why was Alex still being questioned? Surely there wasn't a problem. Surely the police didn't believe Alex was guilty of any crime.

No sooner had the worrisome thought come to her than her cell phone rang. She considered letting it ring but then dismissed the idea. It could be her sister or her parents, eager to know what was going on with her.

She rummaged in her purse and found her phone. Her forehead furrowed when she saw Salina's name flashing on the screen.

"Salina?" Brianne said, putting the phone to her ear. "Is that really you?"

"Hey, Bree," Salina said. "Got your message. What's going on?"

"I'm at a police station in Orlando."

"What?"

"Yep." Brianne spent the next few minutes giving Salina the condensed version of what had happened since Alex had shown up at her door. But she didn't tell her about how she and Alex had connected. That would be a story for when the two friends were together, sharing a bottle of wine.

"Unbelievable," Salina said. "Will you have to testify in court and everything?"

"I guess it depends on what happens now. If Carter pleads guilty or claims innocence." Brianne blew out a huff of air, the idea of having to go to court making her nervous. "But forget about me. What's going on with you? You've been so hard to track down."

"I've just been crazy busy," Salina said. "Feeding New Yorkers is no easy task," she added with a chuckle.

"Maybe I can head to the big city and visit you sometime soon."

"Um . . . sure," Salina said. "After Christmas. I'll let you know when I've got some time."

"Great," Brianne said. But she had the feeling her friend was giving her the brush-off. And not for the first time, she got the feeling that something major was going on with her.

But she didn't get the chance to ask Salina about her life, because when she looked up, she saw Alex.

"Salina, I've got to go. Let's talk soon, okay?"

"Okay."

Brianne pressed the End button on her cell phone. Then she once again looked in Alex's direction.

Her heart began to pound. She was nervous, she realized. The serious look on his face had her suddenly unsure that he wanted anything to do with her. Maybe he had concluded that he needed a break from the stress of the situation.

From her.

Tentatively, she stood. And then Alex smiled.

Relief rushing through her, Brianne rushed toward him and threw herself into his arms.

He wrapped her in an embrace, and Brianne began to cry. The emotion of the day finally got to her.

"Hey," Alex said, easing back when he realized she was crying against his shoulder.

"I'm so sorry," she quickly said. "I shouldn't have taken off. I should have stayed at the house with you. I keep thinking, what if you'd been killed by the time I got back there?"

"But I wasn't killed. I'm here. You're here." He framed her face, a smile forming on his lips. "It's over, Brianne. It's finally over."

"Not if Carter pleads innocent. Then we'll have to go to court —"

"No," Alex stressed. "It's over. Carter confessed. To everything."

"He did?"

"Yes. That means there'll be no need for either of us to testify in court. We can finally move on."

God, he had the sweetest smile in the world. And the sexiest.

"Oh, thank God." Brianne hugged him again.

"I'm sorry," Alex whispered into her ear.

She broke the hug and looked at him. *"You're* sorry?"

"For not being totally honest with you before we came down here. I shouldn't have involved you at all."

"No, don't apologize. I'm glad I came. Because if I hadn't, I wouldn't have realized that I love you."

Alex's eyes lit up. *"Realized?"*

Brianne was silent for a moment, considering the words that had just come from her lips. They surprised her, but she knew without a doubt that they were true.

"Yes," she said, nodding. "I mean that the way it sounded. I think that I always loved you. I . . . I just didn't know it."

Alex circled his arms around her waist. "Music to my ears, baby. Because I've loved you ever since the moment I met you."

His voice was deep and husky, and despite being in a police station, Brianne's body was growing warm with excitement.

"And I want to be your husband," he added.

Brianne's eyes widened as she stared at Alex. "Are you —"

"Serious? I've never been more serious in my life. I believe we were always meant to be together. Carter just got in the way."

"All that matters is that we found our way to each other, even if it was a long and winding path to get to this point."

"We don't have to dwell on the past anymore. We have our future to look forward to."

"Our future." Brianne smiled. "I love the sound of that."

Right there in the police station waiting room, Alex lowered his head and kissed her. A slow, hot, deep kiss that proved the gravity of his feelings for her.

Her body on fire, Brianne broke the kiss and looked up at the man she loved. "Are you ready to leave?"

"Oh, I'm ready," he told her huskily.

Brianne's body tingled. "Then let's not waste another moment. I want to get back to Daytona as quickly as possible."

"So you can have your wicked way with me?"

"Something like that."

Grinning devilishly, Alex lowered his head and kissed Brianne hotly once more. "Oh, man. The hour drive to Daytona is going to be torture."

"Sweet torture," Brianne said. "Think of how the anticipation will build with every single mile . . ."

"I love you," Alex said.

"I love you, too."

Then, taking her hand, Alex led her out of the police waiting room, both of them giddy with excitement.

And ready to express the physical manifestation of a love they knew would last forever.

Kayla Perrin has been writing since the age of thirteen and once entertained the idea of becoming a teacher. Instead she has become a *USA TODAY* and *Essence* bestselling author of dozens of mainstream and romance novels. She has been recognized for her talent, including twice winning Romance Writers of America's Top Ten Favorite Books of the Year Award and the Career Achievement Award for multicultural romance from *RT Book Reviews*. Kayla lives with her daughter in Ontario, Canada. Visit Kayla at www.KaylaPerrin.com.